ENTEL

The Bystander Effect

Library of Congress Control Number: 2025919630

First edition

ISBN (paperback): 979-8-9931339-0-4
ISBN (hardcover): 979-8-9931339-2-8

This book was professionally typeset on Reedsy.
Find out more at reedsy.com

Dedicated to the hues of the soul.

Contents

Eli

How would one know if a damsel is in distress? Is it the screams? The eerie feeling in the air? Or just the blatant vibes you get from the strangeness of strangers? Right now, it's all of the above. With the events unfolding in front of me, I can't disguise the shiver running up my back. This killer is really getting in there. I should leave. Pretend this never happened, because this is not the way my night was supposed to go. Despite the viciousness this victim is experiencing, I can't escape the selfishness of my thoughts. Why me? Why this time? And why, of all days, do I have to be witness to something so vile?

"She isn't technically in distress if she isn't breathing," I whisper. Strike one. That's not funny, E. None of this was funny. Especially, when I could be next up on the chopping block. And this person in navy blue was good. Too talented for this to be an accident. Too resourceful for me to get away, and too good for me to say anything. Should I even say something? Why don't you say something?

I could back away slowly, as the one in blue pulls the lifeless woman's head up from under the basin of water. However, they seem to be taking their time, enjoying the moments between us. She was dead, like really dead, and I'm going to be too if my

1

phone rings. It's a bit late to put it on silent. I'm not even sure what my plan would be if it rang. And instead of focusing on this "whatever" that is front of me, I keep recalling the words Mom told me; not to take shortcuts in life. I assumed she spoke of things figuratively, like all moms do, but now in a grimy alleyway, in downtown Shady Oaks, is where I will meet my demise. Just putting this out there, it would be a real pity if these are my final thoughts to this world.

What should I do, Wisdom? Can I call you that? Since you and I are both witnesses to what is happening in real time? Yes, you, the one watching as I jot my thoughts down and mark them in my brain. I mean you are wise right? Whatever, I think Wisdom is a good name. I wonder what her name was. The woman lying on the frigid ground, still and limp as the killer rolls her body in blue tarp, to put in the trunk of some probably stolen sedan.

I know I should get away but since I am already here with you, answer me this. Why blue? Out of all the tarp colors in the world, why would anyone choose the color blue? This sicko is also wearing blue. Should I be remembering this? Wis, can you remember that for me? Who knows, I might need it later. Against all that blue, their car is abnormally black, with no license plate. The woman, cold, but looking further, I could tell that she was kind. This stuff doesn't happen to bad people, maybe that is why I am here now watching, observing, regretting.

Maybe I am next, and it will be game over. "However, this isn't a game, E." I shake my head, grimacing as I recognize that I am still here with this unaware menace, and should probably call the police. Can't. Phone isn't on silent. My memory just isn't the most reliable when I witness murder.

And I know what you're thinking, just turn it down. Sorry, I can't. When one keeps with the trends, we throw away our most responsible thoughts. So in correct follower fashion, I had to change my keyboard to that typewriter sound everyone has, and unfortunately, it's loud. Too loud for the situation I am in. They haven't seemed to noticed me yet, so maybe I can slip on by.

As Eli takes a small step backwards, the gravel under his toes amplifies upon the tightening brick walls. The killer looks toward the alley opening, alarmed. Missing Eli as he drops to the ground to duck from their view.

Maybe I can cause a distraction, Wis. I mean another one. What would any heroic guy do in this situation? They probably would fight this visceral killer adorned in cobalt. But that's stupid. Also that's just not me; I do wish I had taken a martial arts class when I was younger, but no, my forte is piano. See Dad. Jazz can't save me now. Can you save me, Wisdom? At least you are here with me, in my hopefully, not last moments. I can't die yet. I'm too young and dumb to waste what little life has granted me. I should get behind this trashcan. And by the grace of all things good, I hear the sirens. Whew. Thank goodness for the police. Despite the social turmoil and constant injustice my people face, I am happy to hear that sweet screech coming closer. Does that make me a hypocrite? Don't answer that.

"Police! Put your hands up!" Sighing in relief, Eli pushes his weight from crouching to stand on wobbly legs. Not fully stable yet, he takes a step back, turning attention to the back alleyway. Of course, there is no killer in sight. Just two cops, Elijah, and a cold puddle on the ground where that woman once laid. How could the killer even get away in the car that quickly? The figure in blue. Navy and ghastly. Gone.

—-

"I didn't do anything," Eli dejected. The LED overhead light burns his back as he focuses on the spit landing from the angry officer's mouth onto a spot on the table. "You believe me right?" He adds. "I was just hanging with my friends tonight, left early, and took a quick turn home. Who knew I would see what I saw!"

I mean you were there with me, so why am I in this cold room, with these odd people staring at me like some criminal. I can't help it. These cops are frustrating me, wasting their time and spit on nonsense. Elijah stares at the spit further. It reminds him of the puddle that woman laid in. Her body and blank eyes staring deeply into his soul.

I was there, Wisdom. I have seen murder, and for some reason that doesn't sit right. As if I am tainted now. Wait. Am I a suspect? How could I be? I mean I am not a killer. I even do my due diligence of letting ladybugs out of the house when they get in. Not spiders though, because those are vicious animals. But if anyone asked, I value most life. The thought arises to me that again this only seems to happen to kind people. Because something so cinematic as this can't happen to the bad guys. Character development for those with the strongest endurance. Right?

"Why were you in the alley kid? Do you work with Mr. Q.?"
"Mr. Q.?" So it was a man. Figures. "Sir, who even is that, and why is his name so lame?" Honestly, can that even be considered a name? I guess the cool names were taken. I'm disappointed though, with the Bundys, Dahmers and Zodiacs, Q feels quite lazy. It's just a letter, as if the rest of the name fell off, and it leaves me wanting more. "Furthermore, I was promised a

phone call, and my lawyer will be hearing about this blatant discrimination against the youth."

I don't like where this is going. This isn't good. I'm not sure what route to play, Wis, to show these cops I am not the guy they are looking for. What they are doing is normal in this day and age. The police often shoot first then ask questions, and the fact that I have no holes in me has me thankful that all they did was arrest me. No matter how wrong that is. One fact of the matter is that I was at the scene of the crime. Admittedly, I can't help but wonder why I always seem to get paired up with the old and the odd. Like I was destined to encounter life with those who never even try to see from my lens. As if they weren't informed or full of life to question morals and correctness. That woman would have had morals, she was once full of life. And now she's gone. Q as well. Like an enigma.

"Just answer the question kid. Someone tipped us off. Why were you in the exact location as a notorious killer?" Notorious is rich. Only the police would give such a profound word over to someone who literally kills for unknown reasons. Was it convenience? Maybe she deserved to be dealt with. But who deserves to be drowned? I can't stand the thought of people taking the lives of others into their own hands. To make a decision of murder deep into the night or in the middle of the day. "What makes you think I would associate with such a person? One, I don't have a motive, and two, I want my phone call."

—-

"You believe me right? Good. Now hand it over I won," Eli cheeses, shaking his hand towards his friends to receive compensation.

"Ugh, you always win," sulks Daniel. He's always been a sore loser, ever since we were kids. But he's my best friend and even though I try to take it easy on him, he's a goof that attracts losing. Losing is his trademark to be precise, well at everything except my company, and his girlfriend's. "And now you hand it over." "Fine, but technically you weren't being detained just questioned," ejects Hope. She is so spunky for such a small girl. "Ha. A technicality you say. Whatever, I will enjoy the smell of victory while you haters count your losses." Despite the rift in our personalities, these are my friends. Ill-fated and ill-tempered. My Dad calls us "Il trio de destino," the trio of doom. Old man doesn't even know Italian but swears that all the trouble we find ourselves in transcends languages and cultures. But what can I say they are my second family. The cynical type who love to think that I will lose on one of our wagers, one of these days, but alas that day is not today.

I mean, who knew out of the three of us I would be the first to go to jail, or be arrested. I always suspected it would be Hope, because she's so far left it just feels right. "Alright class, don't forget you have a mid-term coming up." The professor drones over a scattered desk. "Great. Arrests and tests," mutters Daniel. I shake my head in disbelief. Grabbing my bag from the lecture hall floor, I open the zipper and pocket the cash, feeling a pair of eyes on my back. There is something behind me, but as I turn around and look closer towards the window in the corner, all I see is a blur of a shadowy figure passing by. Not catching anything but the color of their shoes.

There it is again Wis, there is that color. What do you make of that? Me? I'm hardheaded, so I'll shake the thought as nothing more than a coincidence to ponder on about for another time.

Q

"Green represents the dead image of life." - Rudolf Steiner

Here lies Damsel number... Well it doesn't matter who came first or who will come last, as my hand executes judgment upon them all. A very chicken and egg scenario. Now I know what you're thinking, what an envious thing, that I could be the one to strip them of breath and all things green. I often rush, and for that, I apologize.

Genuinely, I am sorry for my greed, but who can honestly deny themselves of such freshness and wonder. Impossible really. To take all that the trees can offer. I just help and give my tribute back to nature in the form of early decomposition. Not my decomposition, but you get the point. We'll return to this topic later, okay my friend?

Right now I need you to pay attention to my latest fixation. She had forest eyes and they yearned to be returned to where they belonged. Now let's not get it twisted, I may be a mystery. But is that a crime? I'm no monster. I wouldn't do something so heinous and just bury a body. How wasteful is that, and needlessly egregious if I must say. So if you think I will get caught using a tactic like that then sorry, wrong story, wrong person, wrong time.

I think we should start over. It is best for the both of us, if I rewind us back to a few hours prior, because despite my exterior, I really am no creature of despair. Let me tell you, I was having a good day, great even, just like everyone else. When I am not planning my next plucking, I am residing at my favorite coffee place, the Olive Branch. It's nothing special, just a cute little hole in the wall with the most vile tasting drinks I have ever graced my taste buds upon. Really horrid stuff, and today was like no other. I was standing in line boringly, and that is where I saw her. Who she is doesn't matter, so we'll call her Damsel. A word befitting who she is. And what she is; does, or better yet her overall essence. It was today's color, green. And as I adorned myself in her wave of sage ecstasy, I hadn't noticed the waitress calling my order out. "Matcha latte, hold the foam! Going once, Going twice."

"Wait!" I exclaimed. Hand reaching out to grab onto the last remnants of jade leaving by, not entirely sure who I was grasping for. However, this Damsel was cute. She actually responded to my sudden outburst, surprised even. But as she turned to see who was yelling in her vicinity, I react smarter than that. Quickly grabbing the poison from the cashier, I threw some cash down, paying no mind to the change that halted to the floor, and rushed into a nearby booth.

Let's not be reckless. I have no way of getting caught, but I will not make it easy, simply for the sport of it all. I can't help but think, tapping impatiently on the plush cushion beneath me, that the authorities have been searching for me. Getting caught would put an unpleasant stamp on this story I have built, but I often forget entirely that they are unwise and unwelcome into this marvelous game I created. Such foolish personas humming like leaves in the wind, sniffing every rock in order to find me.

So I refuse to be seen. I can't give them any leeway, it would be a betrayal to my values.

How sneaky this mind of mine is, I almost lost my train of thought. Why can't they move faster? Don't they know that she is next in this game? Can't they feel my stares on her? It is a pity that people are so blind to the world around them. I tell you, I try so hard to be transparent but to no avail. It is impossible for them to imagine, that I have hand-plucked this crowd to be witness, to my next tribute of the upmost sacrifice. They have not the slightest idea.

The chime of the door is made, alarmingly shaking my head back into clarity, and as she saunters off unknowingly, I proceed to toss my untouched vial in the trash, utterly finished with such arduous tasks, like the normalcy of stalking. I must act now, but this phase in the plan is always a gamble. It could take me weeks to pinpoint the exact moment of harvest, and I don't see the sense in bet-making when destiny can fall into my own hard earned efforts. Please believe me, they are hard earned. She deserves it. I walk out of the humid building, looking for a sign from above that I didn't waste my time on her. As I almost give up due to utter impatience, I am pleasantly lulled to see a fully rusted penny roll out the door and into my foot. Oh, I can't help if an idea creeps inward, and my face has a mind of its own, when a smile begs to plague it. I am so transparent it disgusts me, but now I have a method. A gift to the trees and a way to get my forest green.

—-

"Dispatch said they haven't found the body yet, just some clues that led to a bunch of pennies. I think this is another misdirect. I mean, what could it all mean Diaz?" I can't focus. This killer was good, and somehow they are still hidden. Rolling back into my chair, I tap my temple in thought as the voice from across the room alerts me. "Diaz." Calls the Lieutenant. "This is the fifth missing person this month. There doesn't seem to be a matching motive or anything that ties these girls together up with the rest." That's strange. As far as I know, most serial killers have some sort of pattern recognition. It's like an emblem to their craft. That even with having a tell, the authorities can't catch them so quickly. Despite this blatant truth, it is in the job description to think that the many of them deal with some deeper mental issues. I mean something has to be wrong inside for a killer to, you know, kill.

"And they used pennies, not even dimes or nickels for these poor women. Cheap bastard."

"That's not funny, Campbell. They have to mean something; everything left behind has to mean something. They are questioning us, mockingly telling us to keep up." I sigh. This killer was the worst kind of villain. No motive, no connections, just a strange affection towards killing. Like love almost. Death especially in this form should never be a riddle to solve. It does no justice to the families who deserve answers. "Yeah I know." Campbell states, rubbing the back of his neck apologetically.

"I wasn't making a joke. It's just the news won't get off our back and I'm getting fed up. I mean all of us at the station assume its a group behind this. To many killings for it to be one person. But the public is positively convinced it is a man leading this charade. If it is then I can't condone this disrespect to all these women." Campbell isn't wrong. He just gets too caught up in cases like this to think rationally. He is right about the craziness online though.

The internet has always been a ruthless place for subjects like this, but it doesn't help us at all that this "Q" has a cult following online. I mean just because of the nature and severity of these crimes, everyone has written off any woman of being the main suspect behind all this. I can expect this from civilians but when did the police get so reckless in thinking? "Matt, take a look at this photo of pennies lined up in a question mark. No one in the forest, no traces left behind either. How does this Q. person even do it?"

Campbell has a point. We really don't know the slightest thing about this criminal. No leading description, no name, no face to pair with this crime, so the public fed up with the police's slowness, have began calling them Mr. Q. Even if I think that's a little forward to gender this crime, I have to admit that this does have the city on high alert, which has been some amount of help. I mean, I still don't understand the national high people get on fictionalizing real killers with silly names, but now the police have a path to adhere to. I guess we have "Q.'s" rising influence to thank for that.

"That's it!" I exclaim, erratically jumping out of the desk chair.

"What, have you found our guy?" "Or gal." I interject. "Right," nods Campbell.

"But to answer your question, no, but I have a hunch." "You always have a hunch." Shushing Campbell with my outstretched hand I notion that he needs to pay attention. "No Campbell, look. What do forest and pennies have to do with each other? They are, or rather turn green. They age and rust and can provide life and death. Not so much a penny, but you get it, right?" I hope I'm on the right track here. "Green," smiles Campbell. "They are green, what is that stuff on pennies called again?" He asks into his smartphone. "Verdigris." I state before his search assistant can.

He used verdigris and poisoned that woman. Where can one even find a load of that? "And that doesn't answer where the body is, or the motive," I huff as I dejectedly slide back into my chair again. Campbell pats me on the shoulder, his face directed towards the door. "Well as you continue to think, I have to speak to a suspect related to this whole matter down the hall. Lewis is probably trying to intimidate them. That old bat really needs to retire," He chuckles opening the door. "Anyway, keep me posted on your progress Diaz."

"Will do, thanks Lieutenant." I nod. "Detective." He nods back at me, before shutting the door. As he proceeds to wind down the hall towards the interrogation room. Focusing back on my notes in front of me, I scribble the word *green* down in my journal, and shut my eyes, trying not to lose the thoughts between my ears. Outwardly whispering, "I will find you Q. And unfold every question you leave behind." With that I open my eyes once more and face towards the computer, zoning out as the door down the hall opens, and a voice loudly in the distance says; "One, I don't have a motive, two, I want my phone call, and three, he was wearing blue, navy blue."

Wisdom

"Can't you see? Well, I can see it all; and it had to be you Wisdom." The damsel in the chair squirmed and muffled a scream under the sunshine duct tape. "How interesting, I can feel the warmth emanating from within you. And as it burns so, it leaves me dying of thirst my love." With an unoccupied hand Q. wiped a noticeable tear caressing the cuts and bruises painting her cheeks. He paid no further mind to the girl pulling at the rope, tugging at her occupied wrists.

"Huh," he states confusingly at her disfigured form, "I didn't want to hurt you yet, but you left me no choice. I abhor when people interrupt me. It is a rather rude habit to adopt." The man, now donning an amber sweater, paced, took a far skip and landed deep into the sand, excitedly. Mood swinging with his movements.

"I am having too much fun!" He twirled. "Aren't you happy Wisdom? Can I see that sunny smile? For you give my awful world color. It's like I said before, I hate when people interrupt my space, my plans, and my peace.

Now, I know it is a little risky to kill someone at the beach, for onlookers can find me. But I am transparent, and I like tempting fate, other than the fact that no one will catch me, they lack resolve. And like my dear Wisdom here, I see more than meets the eye."

The damsel began to realize that she wasn't going to make it by the end of this moment, so as the rays pined harder on her and the heat feverishly peeled at her skin, she allowed herself to breakdown into a most justified sob, relentlessly trying harder to pull on the ropes holding her back. "I will amuse you," chimed Mr. Q, as he ripped the restraint clenching the skin around her lips.

"But as I give you a fighting chance, please, my dear Wisdom listen to this tragic tale." "My name isn't Wisdom! Sir, I don't know what I did wrong but-," she sputters, but Mr. Q. frustrated with her voice put the tape back onto her screaming, shaking his head disappointingly. "I told you that I am not pleased to be interrupted and you must listen before your golden end arrives. Now as all backstories begin, I will tell you the tale of my childhood. I am an orphan. I'm sorry, I lied, I'm not, but with a mother like mine, I made it so.

She was a person like you, Wisdom, often embellished in self-righteousness, and through her visceral doctrine, chose to dish up judgment. Now this judgment was based upon what she saw and what she heard." Mr. Q focused and sat in the warm sand and drew a question mark on the ground. Face strewn in a sea of discontent.

"She, like most people in this rainbow cesspool of a world, had something wrong with her. I don't know if it was the fact that my father departed early, or that her cards were simply dealt badly, but I was not the ace she had hoped for. Maybe I was her Jester, like the guy that dons clown attire and fights the villain in black," he uttered.

"Nonetheless, her gift of seeing colors as those around her spoke their words into existence, made her feel as if she obtained a superpower. But there was a weakness to being special, too hot to touch, aflame on display because of me, Wisdom."

He shockingly grabbed the Damsel. "Pay Attention!" The victim froze in fear, eyes locked onto the masked man and of what would be coming next. Disappointingly, Q. grabbed a solid object from his bag of goodies, and stuck it into the nearby bonfire. A few seconds later, she writhed in pain as a branding iron scorched into her fleshly back, eliciting a wail from her covered lips; the only thing hiding her muffled screams for help. As her hot tears fell and her breath began to shallow, the man in the blond garb pulled her in and laughed before throwing her head back and standing up.

"Now the real kicker was the teachings she laid upon me. Most days she was who knows where, neglectful, dismissive. But one day, it turned for the worse. I was being innocent, as I always was, because I am no monster, no villain. Minding my own business, doing as children desire to do, I decided to sing. Just a small, simple tune the world has conditioned us to recite like a prayer:

Twinkle, twinkle, little me.

And I guess my mother decided I was too much. She grabbed me by the neck and held me close, to the point that all the color rushes to my face. Red, blue, yellow, you know the primary colors. And of course, I cry out to her. But what gets me to shut up, to stop interrupting her once and for all," he whispers into the Damsel's ear, pulling her closer to listen as his warm breath makes her jump with every syllable enunciated. "Is when she turns to me and says; I can't see it. You hold no color. You have no place."

Mr. Q paces the floor, anger rising to him as he remembers

this tale. He jumps to the side and kicks some sand in the direction of the victim, causing her to flinch. "This was the usual occurrence after a while, I have felt her kicks and punches, and dealt with broken bones to satiate her disgust with me. But I thought it was a way of showing love. Most mothers love their children. Don't you love yours?" The woman drops her head and sobs, shaking violently at this point.

"But," he stammers, "Wisdom, her telling me that I have no color was the heartbreaking point. I HAVE COLOR! Don't I? Ha. I guess not," he chuckled.

"But I am wise, smart, adaptable. So one night, I decided she saw and felt too much. All that fire and warmth I mistook as love from the wretched witch, I took it back and... Well I won't tell you what happened next, I'm no monster, so I'll spare the details," he laughed. Drawing this woman in for the nth time, baiting her with terror. "But just like the sun, darling, my mom, who my world orbited. You too are getting on my nerves. and I decided it is time for your end." The damsel began to cry silently now, head falling hopelessly low.

"Oh, don't shed tears, I hear there is a light to see at the end of the tunnel, and yellow it gives and yellow it shall receive," he spat as he grabbed a shell from the ground and pierced the damsels' neck muttering, "Wisdom. Wisdom."

He stood up, disregarding the sunken woman, as heat escaped from her nape, spilling the rest of her gold onto the molten sediment. He strode to the black car, no license plate, and threw the bloodstained shell into the trunk. "Can others see you? Can you hear them as well? Are they special too? Or am I colorlessly alone, Wisdom?"

—-

"Guys, we can't go, We have that mid-term exam tomorrow,

remember? I gotta study, or my parents will drive up here and wonder why I didn't make Varsity," Eli spoke, as his friends dropped their cheers and turned to him angrily.

"First, you won't tell us what you got arrested for. Now, we can't go to the beach to hang out like usual. We already missed out three weeks ago. What next, you have imaginary friends you talk to?" chimed Hope. "Pfft, yeah right. The only friends he has are us. Because that would be messed up, E. Also everyone knows studying the night before is bogus." I can't tell them Wis, you understand, that it's just me that talks to you? As Eli turns to face his friends he pulled a coin out of his hand and tossed it in the air. Hoping an appropriate excuse could come to him in this moment to sway his friends. Whilst midair, Daniel snatched it and gave it a twirl in his hands. "Where did you find such a dusty penny?"

Before E could grab it back, Hope interjected, "That's really gross guys. Don't you know you can catch diseases from touching that stuff?" "Right," Daniel agrees, throwing the coin to the ground. "Bro, that was mine," Eli annoyingly mentions, reaching for the change discarded to the floor. "I found it in front of some cafe." Just as Eli picks it up, he can't help but get some of the residual rust on his fingers. I wonder what this stuff is, do you know Wis?

"I heard that all that rust can give you tetanus," voices Daniel. "My sister told me it makes your fingers turn yellow," adds Hope. "Thanks for that guys." Eli sighs throwing the penny in the trash and wiping his hands on his pants, leaving streaks of evidence behind. "I don't want to be sun-stained." "Nice!" Daniel adds, throwing a wad of paper near E, missing the trashcan entirely. "Then you would really be the golden boy everyone thinks you are."

Diaz

"I hate the rain." That's why I moved out here, for warmer days where the hours, minutes, and seconds aren't all meshed. Despite the weather, Shady Oaks is entirely too bleak in spirit and miserable and gray and… never mind. There's no point in stressing over the cons, in a town I swore to protect. There are too many lives to save. Real people who don't want to hear about how visceral my mornings can be, or how I might want to offer my talents in the form of anything else.

Despite my efforts, there is no use in trying to uplift my soul when the city does nothing but take. I think what irks me is that I don't know what the right thing to do is. As a detective, that's merely taking a joke of the clues and beating the criminal to the punchline. But lately I have been behind. Almost as if the joke is entirely on me.

"Diaz, my office," calls Campbell. "Roger that." I declare, tossing the soaked overcoat haphazardly across a chair, disregarding the puddle forming underneath it on the ground. As I shuffle into the poorly lit office, Campbell gestures to a file on the desk.

"I know this was under the eyes of James last, but I said if anyone could catch this sicko it would be you," he voices. "We all know that this is beyond what the Captain thinks. Honestly,

I don't know if he would give this up to anyone. The more we uncover clues the more this seems out of SOPD jurisdiction. But I argued and chose you, because you see him, don't you?" "See him?" I shift. Can I see him? I know I want to catch this guy, but not at the cost of Campbell's career. That's too risky.

"My reputation precedes me, I guess. Can't promise anything." This is different, unachievable. And to be honest I shouldn't consume myself with work. "Third serial killer type in the area within the last ten years, and despite the gall of the other two. This one is something else. No motive, no face, just questions." Campbell acknowledges my response by flipping his briefcase open, pointing at the question marks appearing in various printed pictures. I grab a photo as he pauses, waiting for me to take the bait. "What's this?" I interject.

"That my friend is why you are here; no one can make sense of this one. If we don't solve this then the FBI will swoop in. But I digress. In this photo there is an amalgamation of items found at the scene of the crime. Red liquid, blue paint, separated by a question mark made of ash-colored pebbles. I know I shouldn't be saying this but as our last resort, what can you make of it?"

I know Campbell is saying this to reel me in but little does he know, I am already intrigued. "I take it our guy can't color within the lines," I chuckle out, uneasy by the lack of answers in front of me. "I do like the choice of color, coincidence?" I ask, turning to the man questioning my skills. "Come on, Matt. What do you really see? I'm not Cap or Lewis, or some other guy just expecting to spell it all out. What do you make of this mess?" Startled by his desperate question, I give up on laughter and look at the serious person now in front of me, realizing that I am indeed a last resort here, being tested before this case turns rigid like metallic frost. Once this gets out of local hands, who knows when the mystery of "Q." will be solved.

"Well, you think these things hold no importance, but they all coincide. You see that red stuff looks like bromine, and is very poisonous. The blue paint, or what we all think is paint, is probably some form of cyanide liquidized, also poisonous, and the pebbles. Did Forensics find them painted?"

"How did you know?" asks Campbell, impressed with my deduction skills. "I was a Chemistry major before the Academy, but that's not important. To continue my thoughts, this I am certain has to be silver, pharmaceutical-grade, dusted on these rocks." "Of course my ace of a detective is correct. Forensics just got the results this morning." Campbell added. "It's shiny, almost alluring, and also poisonous," I add. But what would a killer want with three poisonous chemicals, when one could do the job just fine?

"Yeah, I figured you'd get that much. This was picked up at the abandoned paint warehouse downtown. Thought I'd brief you before sending you out to dig further, but you know everything I wanted to tell. That at least leaves us more time to brainstorm further in the car." The Lieutenant closes the file and walks towards the door.

"Technically, it was to go further up the chain, but I thought it would be rude not to tell you, given your history." A flicker of pain dawns on me. What could that mean? I know he isn't referring to what happened back then. Or is he? Not trying to show the hurt forming, I blink back and smirk at Campbell. "Don't go getting soft on me John," punching his shoulder. "Save that for the bad guys," Campbell says, jokingly rubbing his arm. "I will catch up with you later and meet you there. I forgot Cap told me to share your findings with him." "Alright. I'll fill you in when I am done there then. Thanks, Campbell."

"Sure, and be careful, I know you just got back from a break. You're the only one I have left. That means something." The only one left, huh? I try not to remember that. I try not to get in my head about the past, but with Campbell on my back, I can't help but tighten my holster and think of what occurred. What I could have done differently, and ever since that time, every day becomes harder to focus in on. As if I am living as smoke. Hollow and aimless. I miss before then. I miss them.

—-

The smell of mildew and pigment wafts as the crate-like doors open. "This way, Detective, here is the scene," a scientist gestures. "Thanks, anything else turned up since the last report?" "Nothing, the perpetrator was thorough, to say the least."

As the lab coat walked off, I crouch low to the ground, beginning to touch one of the vibrant rocks. Gloved, of course, because if it is poison painted, that would spell trouble. Examining further, this stone feels off. I notice that it isn't just some rock but rather a piece of charcoal. Now that's interesting.

"I don't understand," whispering to myself. "What is the purpose of this?" Turning back to the people checking for other clues, I exclaim over the loud machinery. "You sure there is nothing else? This can't be the only thing, I know I'm good, but come on, I'm no super genius." The forensic scientist looked up from the notebook, "I don't know, man, I just find the clues and run the tests. Isn't it your job to make sense of it all?"

Diaz, frustrated by the lack of effort, walks over to the table. "Tell me, what would happen if this stuff got on your hands or skin?" "Well, it could be highly corrosive, but a crazy thing happens when you mix cyanide and bromine," the scientist comments. "When those two interact, they can either release an odorless gas or a white solid. Varies depending on the dosage of each" Odorless and white, huh? How strange for it to be placed next to charcoal, something so staining and strong, as if the barrier is combining to create-

"Smoke." Diaz realizes the importance of it all and heads near the door to call the Lieutenant. "Campbell, it's smoke, it's a smokescreen, a misdirection. The killer is misleading us to get us off his odorless scent. I got it!"

"Got what?" Questions Campbell. "Diaz, just get back here and we'll sort things out."

"Right, I'll be there in a few. Let me see if I can catch a cab." With no car in sight to be seen, Diaz snatches his coat and runs out the door. "Hey, what about the rain?" yells the Scientist. Diaz, set on departure, turns his head. "What about it, it's just water, scared it won't wash the sins away?" He chuckles before heading out the door.

"Sins, more like evidence", mutters the annoyed Examiner, unaware of a hole in the roof of the decrepit building, sharing its wet gift upon the substances on the floor, pooling it into a hue of disaster.

—-

"Thanks for the ride," mouths Eli, handing over a ten-dollar tip. Rejecting his offer, the masked driver of the black car, license plate, whispers, "Keep that my friend. here's a tip instead. Don't take shortcuts in life. The long journey might be the destination."

"I think my mom said something like that before." "Wise woman," states the driver. "Right, thanks man," E shrugs as he closes the door. The driver pulls off, staring through the rear view at the trio of friends narrowing near the door of the abandoned building.

"So what are we doing here, Daniel?" Asks Eli. "I heard there was some stuff left behind, school is too expensive to look down on the gifts of thrifting." "You mean stealing. This might be someone's building still," nudges Hope, irritated that she was dragged out on a weekday night.

"If someone lived here, they might need to 'thrift' more than we do," laughed E. As they pushed the creaky doors open, the trio began to look around. "Um. I don't think we are the first people here," added Hope. "Why do you say that?" asks Eli, now seeing the police tape. Daniel walks to where E is and stops in awe. "Come check it out! E found something cool."

On the ground, the three witness a phenomenon of bleeding color intertwined into the deepest tint, engulfing the path of charcoal shaped into the line of a question. "What is it?" "I don't know, looks sick though," crouches Daniel. "Let me see," Eli insists, moving in forward for a better view, just as the streaks and tears of white and violet speak to him. And as if an eternity has transpired he hears a voice and whispers back into the void.

"Wisdom."

Violet

"Imagine if you died right now. I would be highly disappointed." The man in plum shoes paced across the creaky floor, shaking his head in a mix of emotions, mostly disgust. "Just as you took my breath away, from the moment I saw you, I knew I needed to take yours. The Damsel clawed at her neck, asphyxiating with the lack of oxygen, yearning for freshness as the colorless cloud held her further into the smoke.

"I'm urging you to let out some noise. Scream for help. Cry!" He exclaimed, taunting the Damsel as she tried to open her muted airways, ultimately failing into further desperation. It didn't help that she had no form of escape from this psycho. That the pain rose to a peak until her tears began singeing her eyes; such an innate response was causing far more suffering than relief. Such duality like red and blue.

"When I saw you, I was intrigued, for I never knew a person could possess two colors," Mr. Q. giggled. "I know what you're thinking. Why me? Oh, I should have stayed home. Someone I love will worry about me. Do they know I am missing? How can I get out of this? Blah, Blah, Blah." This part of the job never amused him, He would rather spend the time torturing and giving his excerpts from the past. But Q. possessed an almost respect for routine and obligation, despite the boredom it caused him.

Turning on his heels, he pulled his mask up a little to get a quick whiff of the substance plaguing the victim. The high went straight to his head clearing his sinuses immediately. Through a stifled cough he continued. "Whew! That's some strong stuff. I'd hate to have to breathe that in. Am I right?"

Comedy was never his strong suit, but he loved the sport of it. "Am I a monster? I don't think I am. Sorry, no. For my darling Wisdom, monsters act on impulse. But for me, this is art. A canvas to display how I am rectifying the world because we shouldn't be confuddled with the lack of creativity. My motives are quite simple. People waste their color. So I decided I should clean it up a little. Strip them of their soiled talents in place for something taciturn and right.

"Don't worry, my damsel. Or should I say damsels, it will be over soon. I know it is wrong to pick a victim that holds more than one life force, but I am greedy, sue me. However, before your regal end arrives, can you humor me a little?" He grabbed the chair of the tied woman, and pulled her in the direction of a broken window. Tightening the rope around her wrists, he forcefully pushed her head towards the window, not minding the speed of which he moved, not allowing her to catch a glimpse of breath. It was all the same to him if she gained air or not.

"Now I know one shouldn't mix business with pleasure, and for that, I have brought you near this window for some peace, as a penalty to me.

But Violet, oh royal Violet, you called that cab. You see, you requested me. Is it really my fault that I was the one who feasted upon your hue, knowing that destiny was favoring my hand instead of yours?"

He pushed the chair further, glass centimeters away from scratching her face. "You see, look, there are all those people outside, minding their business, unaware of the danger you and your little one are in.

How selfish of them, right? Such wasps busily coasting along without a care for justice. Only when it hits them do they often feel the sting of life." In my opinion, that is lower than low, Wisdom. "What rodents they are, so happy, so ignorant."

He scoots the chair closer to the bubbling beaker on the table, smoke hitting the woman once more in the face. "Anyway, where were we? Ah. I can't keep forgetting about you and your bundle of joy," he mocks as he rubbed the stomach of the Damsel menacingly. As the motion continued she shut her eyes, violated beyond words.

"What was their name going to be?" She gurgles her words, trying to say something, but nothing comes out. "Fine, don't say anything, how rude to ignore others." Mr. Q saunters in his lilac hat, tipping it towards the victim staring at him like a deer caught in headlights.

"Don't I look nice? I tried to dress for the occasion. Right, no talking, sorry," he laughs. "Don't worry, it will all be over soon, then I will have to deal with cleaning you up too. The world is selfish, but my job is like how all janitors live. Thanklessly."

The woman slumps and alarms Mr. Q out of his eclectic thoughts. What a pity. Wisdom, I guess, even I can make mistakes. The dosage was too high. She died before I could finish my monologue.

So selfish.

—-

Wisdom.

"What was that, E?" inquires Hope.

"Nothing, nothing!" He exclaims louder than he anticipated. "This is some freaky stuff. Even I don't want to touch it." Eli got up and grabbed a paint can from a corner to sit on. Daniel and Hope grabbed some near them, sitting with him in like fashion. "So what are we doing here, Daniel?" Eli asks. "Well, I thought we could look for hideouts, you know, a place for us to hang."

"And an abandoned warehouse full of paint supplies, that was once a crime scene for an unknown serial killer, mind you, was your first idea?" Questions Hope. "No, I'm not dumb, this was plan B. I was going to choose the beach, but Eli told me they closed it for renovations or something." Elijah shifts in his makeshift seat, not quite looking at the two, but sticking onto the word renovation. Is it okay that I lied to them?

"Also, some history or maybe stats guy said that a killer isn't willing to go back to the place they've offed people, since the police have already searched there. Basic for precautions against getting caught." "Obviously," chimed E. "Still, it's dumb, what if they wanted the police to come, or are waiting for idiots like us to do the easy part for them. All they have to do is kill us now, while we sit and dissect the actions of a weirdo. Also, this place is mega creepy, let's just go," pleads Hope. They all nod in agreement. The trio decides that it is for the best to leave, pondering to themselves about the world of crime and the various motives of modern villains.

—-

"Yeah, Daniel, we shouldn't go to the beach. They seem to be fixing it up and stuff. Some community clean-up project," Eli mutters into the phone. "How much does a beach need fixing? It's just sand and water E." Daniel argues. "I don't know man, the government is weird." He urges, hanging up, turning his attention back down at the puddle of images on the floor. A pool of red; blood unbeknownst to him at that time, splattered strangely and surrounded by a circle of yellow paint.

"I don't know what it is." He speaks back into his device nervously. "See, this is why I told you to go to the library with your friends. Just don't touch or leave anything behind. Good job on calling me first," stresses Eli's Dad on the phone.

"I will come pick you up, and when I get there, we'll think about what to do and who to call. Maybe the police and a lawyer. Again, Elijah, don't touch anything. I mean it."

"Alright, thanks, Dad." Eli obediently replies before ending the call. He backs away slowly, erasing his footsteps in the sand to cover his tracks. As he sits on the curb waiting for his Dad, a black car, with no license plate, drives off in the distance.

Rain

"Who in their right mind kills a woman nine months pregnant?" Questions Campbell, shocked by the sight in front of him. Diaz wasn't listening, he was too focused on keeping his breath steady, trying his hardest not to pass out from the massacre. He swallowed thickly whilst trying to reel in his composure enough to collect more clues.

"Diaz. Diaz, are you alright?" Campbell worriedly inquired. "I know what this means for you. Maybe we should put someone else over the case," he sympathetically offered. "You're zoning out on me. Don't force yourself to fight this battle." He insisted. "I'm fine," Diaz grits.

"If I can't handle it, I will tell you," he states, not fully convincing Campbell one bit. Before Campbell could start an argument, another officer stepped into the frame. "Detective Diaz, this was addressed towards you," he states, passing a black envelope to him.

"Hmm, wonder what this is," Thinking its nothing more than thanks from the old lady he helped earlier that morning with her cat, he places the letter in his jacket pocket and scoots down to collect a sample from the poor woman's body. The victim in front of him was covered in a plethora of burns. That's how he knew to find her in the first place.

"Campbell, it's smoke, it's a smokescreen, a misdirection. The killer is misleading us to get us off his odorless scent. I got it!"

From that, he gathered that the victim would be in a place with a fire, or one that represented the heat. What better place than the abandoned fire station on Thirty-Seventh Street? When the police arrived with paramedics, the building was ablaze, and it took two tedious hours to put the flames out. Once they got inside, they were shocked. The woman found was presumed dead before the fire even began. Further proving that the killer was a sick person because he didn't even have to burn her. Or her dead child.

"I can't take this," Diaz exclaimed a few minutes later, walking to the other side of the room, face drawn of all its color. Amid his impending meltdown, the letter had slipped out of his pocket. Campbell grabbed the object off the floor, signaling Diaz to ask if he minded it being open. Diaz shrugged, not caring what the contents inside contained.

After a few moments, Campbell fell silent, a scared expression creeping across his face as he urged Diaz to take the letter. Diaz protested. "Campbell, I don't feel up to reading fan mail." Campbell urged him, voice going a decibel higher than normal. "I don't care if I have to sit you down myself, read the letter." He was serious, placing the letter on Diaz's chest forcefully. This shocked the Detective, because Campbell was never this adamant on anything. As he grabbed the letter, he opened it slowly, not sure if he was ready to see the black that would haunt him. The letter read:

To the dearest Diaz,

I was there that night, like every night, everywhere all at once. I was chosen. Fortunately for you, I was an angel that day. The mule that carries a load of burden and chance to its destination. Are you confused? So was I when I realized that our fates went beyond these petty crimes and faceless murders. Riddle me this. Doesn't this scene remind you of anything?

Look up and scan the room. My energy is all around. I urge you to take in the smell and the images before you, because it reminded me of your untimely descent from all things happy and honed. How a decision of your own making burned your future.

Diaz looked around, heart racing, not fully trusting his body with such an anxious feeling. Quickly scanning the room for a reaction to indicate if this was a prank gone too far. Woozily, he decided to take a seat, proceeding to continue the cryptic letter.

Rain. That was what you're child's name would have been, right? Pity. Like I told you, I was there that night. Your wife called me. Asking for me to hurry to her need because you were nowhere to be found. How does it make you feel that you gave your all to a job that took away the only thing you couldn't obtain? A goodbye. So here lies a symbolic gift.

Say goodbye to this Damsel and her child. Just like you wished to do for your wife and unborn baby. I would say I am remorseful for you, but you threaten all I build. I pity you, Detective. I am sorry that the last hope your wife and Rain had was me in their time of need. But I could offer them no consolation as I have my own family to tend to.

Unfortunately,
  Mr. Q.

P.S.
  Rain is such an ugly color. You really have a way of cursing the things you create. How gray.

Diaz stood abruptly, letter falling, dropping the chair behind him with a thud. Campbell gave him a sad look, forcing him to realize that everything he just read was real and vivid. Confirmation of the worst form. "Come with me!" He yanked Campbell and pulled him outside.

"How could he have known? No one knows! I, you, she? This is impossible John. Am I the reason this woman and her child died today?" Diaz was hyperventilating, on the verge of hitting anything to let some emotion out. Campbell just stared, contemplating his words, carefully before he slowly began to talk.

"Matt. Matthew. I know what my sister meant to you. Hell, I was going to be an uncle, but you. You lost out on being a Dad and a Husband. And this sicko is taunting you, bragging about his complexes, as if he had a say in the way things went."

Diaz lets out a shaky breath he didn't realize he was holding. "I have to do the right thing, don't I? I have to hand this over to the Captain and explain how this poor woman and child are dead because a serial killer is obsessed with me."

Campbell lowers his head before slightly nodding. "I know you wish for nothing but catching the Bastard, but sit down, process your thoughts, and tomorrow come to me with your answer. Okay? If you want, I can tell Cap."

Diaz nodded, not fully taking in all his Brother-in-law said, just staring at the covered corpse.

—-

Back at home, Diaz didn't bother to close the door or even turn on the lights. He just stood there amidst the dusty terrain, reeling in the what-ifs. What if he was wrong. What if he deserved all that was coming to him. In the past when those thoughts arrived he shook his head. No one can control that kind of death. Thoughtlessly, he began to walk around, stepping on an old toy. It would have been Rain's; he would have been four this year. Tall, probably, like him. Not afraid of the world, for he would have had Diaz the mighty detective to his aid. And his wife. She would be here.

Feeling as if all the emotion was rising within him, he couldn't take it anymore, and threw his keys at the fireplace, hitting the photo he took of his wife when they first heard the news of their bundle to be. Consequently, it fell, glass cracking on the ground with his heart.

Diaz, utterly broken, walked solemnly to pick up the frame. He had no mind of the sharp glass cutting his hand, but stared at himself within the picture. When was the last time he smiled like this? Sincerely, or even had a heartfelt laugh, or spent a night not thinking of what his life could have been if he just picked up the phone that night?

—-

"Call me if you need anything," Matthew said to his wife, Gia, before grabbing his coffee and heading out the door in a rush. She blew him a kiss and chuckled as she proceeded to look at the patches of paint samples on the wall. There were so many variants of gray that one could choose to paint elephants and rain clouds before they all seemed the same.

Rain was a homage to the day they met. She shined so bright

and pure like white upon a dark canvas. And on that particular day, it was a rough one for him. Bad and blackened. But when he saw her within the pour, he knew he had found peace. So they decided to name their little one Rain, to show that love could wash the sadness away.

Gia, not completely sold on the choice of color in front of her, texted her husband asking if he thought it was a good idea to hit up the paint shop for another sample. Diaz always mentioned how blue was cliche, so now gray was their color of choice. His black life and her white love to create a world of gray.

He blindly answered okay, and off she went to the paint store. As she was on the way to return home, the floods opened, and it was time for Rain to arrive. Gia called Diaz, but as he was fairly new at his promoted Detective status, he agreed to a last-minute priority mission.

Panicked and alone, Mrs. Diaz phoned a cab, waddled in, and frantically spoke the address of the hospital to the man behind the wheel. "I don't think that's a good idea. Lady, that hospital is kinda far from us. Like an hour or so. You sure you will be okay back there?" asked the quizzical driver.

"Yes." She erratically spoke in between sharp breaths. "This is where my Husband agreed. His job is closer, so he could visit more often from work, in case something like this ever happened." The driver nodded. "Okay, dial him. No man wants to miss the birth of their child. I know I didn't when my wife had my boy." She reached back into her purse and phoned her love.

No answer.

Ring. Ring. Ring.

No answer.

"You have a son?" She asked, trying to take her mind off

the escalating situation, as her contractions quickened in the backseat. "Yes. He takes after my wife, he is very kind and inquisitive. What about you, what will this one be?"

"It's a boy. My Husband decided on the name Rain. I really like it, it sounds impactful, powerful even; like thunder. Yet quiet like the moments after."

Ring.

No Answer.

Pulling up to the Maternity ward, the car slowed to a stop. "Well, we're here. Do you want me to help grab your stuff?" "Please and thank you." She handed him more than the bill amounted to and squeezed his hand in thanks as he helped her out of the car. As she rushed to the entrance, a small elephant had fallen out of her bag. She hadn't even noticed due to being rushed by the doctors around her. The taxi driver mentioned it to her. She whipped her head back towards the man holding the stuffed animal. All she could muster was reaching her hand back towards him, gesturing for it. It was important to her despite the rising pain; a gift she wanted to present to her child.

"Here," the man offered, handing her back the plush item. "Thanks. Actually if you have time, can you hold on to that for me?" She gasped, before the hospital room door shut. As further events ensued within the room, a nurse excitedly scribbled Gia & Rain on the board hanging next to the door.

Hours went by, and still there was no Detective Diaz. The cab man stared as time slowly crept on. Each second solidifying that he was the only one there for her. After what felt like a long moment, the same nurse returned from inside the room, took a deep sigh, and erased the names sadly from the whiteboard before sauntering off.

The man knew in that moment and held his head low. There

was nothing to say. Everyone had failed her. Leaving her stranded and alone to face the afterworld. The driver took a deep breath of dejection and placed the now sullen elephant on the lobby counter before walking away.

—-

Diaz remembered what happened next when he had got off of work. He checked his phone that night and saw all of the texts and calls his wife had sent him. Then there was nothing for a while.

Afraid of what he thought in his head to be true, especially from the lack of answers anyone around him could give. He walked into the hospital doorways, down the long-winded hall, and froze as he saw the elephant on the table. Lonely and misplaced.

He didn't dare to believe it, and walked into the room slowly, shocked to find his love and his heart covered in white cloth. His feet no longer reacted well, and as he began to fall, the world around him fell dark once again.

—-

As Diaz awoke from this tormenting dream he often had, he wasn't even aware that he fell asleep. In that moment he realized that he wouldn't quit. He couldn't. Not when everything he prized his life upon was gone in a flash. What more could he honestly lose. So as he put on his uniform and stared at the walls half gray with paint swatches, he kissed the cracked photo lopsidedly on the mantle and checked his phone.

Messages from that day were still there as he never changed his number. This was all he had of Gia, and he felt as if it was retribution for his past mistakes to keep the texts. He let out a shaky breath and swiped back from his love's frantic cries for help and dialed Campbell's number.

"I'm not done yet. Let's catch this psycho."

Accomplice

"And that, my friends, is the tour. Despite popular belief, they will let you have a second call based on good behavior." "Come on, kid, stop with the games. Cops still have a few questions to ask you," a dejected officer urges. Eli mutters, annoyed with the sudden interruption, "I guess you will have to tune in next time for Eli's Escapades," before putting his phone away.

"Lead the way." He insisted. After a minute's walk, he and the officer entered back into the interrogation room, Eli wasn't surprised to see Detective Lewis waiting for him. Again. I told you, Wisdom, they always stick me with the old ones. After taking a seat, the cops began. "Alright, Mr. Elliot, before your parents get here, can you continue where you left off?" asks Lewis. "Sure, since you asked so nicely," Eli continued, shifting in his chair. "I was walking back from hanging out at the movies with my friends. It was shutting down so we went for one last hurrah."

"What did you see there?" "A slasher. I'm the fidgety type at horror. So, I figured I saw enough and left earlier than my friends. Who knew I would encounter one on the way home." The cop grimaced, not fully sold on his answer. "Okay, and?" "And? That's it. Saw some guy in blue drowning some lady. Cops came, the killer ran, and now I am here. Did you get all of that?" He asked annoyingly to the other office writing everything down. "Can I go?" "And that's all that happened?" questioned the detective. "Yes, that's all. Man, you're hard of hearing."

"So what about you being at the beach, near another crime scene? Very convenient I must say." Shoot. I forgot about that Wis. What should I even tell them? Eli shifted once again in his chair, becoming increasingly aware of how uncomfortable it was, unsure what to say without blaming two murders on himself, even if he had no part in them. "I-"

Before he could get a word out edgewise, the door bangs open, with Eli's lawyer gesturing for him to go outside, shaking their head at the audacity of the police. "My client has nothing to say. Or must I remind you Lewis, what your jurisdiction is again?" The lawyer handed Eli his bag, speaking closely in his ear before closing the door. "Elijah, your parents are waiting for you in the front. Please refrain from talking to anyone else. I mean it."

Of course. Everyone keeps telling me to shut up. And honestly I'm a little offended, Wis. As E puts his bag on his shoulders and begins walking back towards the entrance where his parents were, he bumped into a familiar face. "Shoot, my bad man, gotta watch where I am going, am I right?" He chuckled, picking his now fallen bag off the floor. "Huh? Yeah, sure, sorry, kind of in a rush." Spoke the figure.

The speedy detective hurried down the way, staring at the files in his hand before opening the door. "Hey Lewis, did that kid leave yet? I had a few questions to ask him," implores Diaz. "Yeah, the jerk. He was just here, surprised you missed him, he never stops talking. Hard to not hear him," lets out the opposing officer. "Okay. Know where I can find him? This is kinda important."

Lewis now fed up with all the questions being thrown at him huffs and gets up. "Just go and get the contact info they left at the front. As a detective, you need to shape up. Goodness Diaz."

—-

A shadowy figure passes by, and I can't catch anything but the color of his shoes. Blue. There it is again Wis, there is that color. "I don't think stalking is allowed on campus. Blue shoes. Might have to let security know I'm being followed." There was no replies to Eli's statements. He huffed in annoyance. "Come on, man, you're not exactly hiding." Eli fed up now, paused his walking, not sure if he should try to entertain the person behind him.

The figure stopped and laughed. "Sharp kid, the name's Diaz. I had a few things to ask you." Diaz flashed his detective badge at Eli, trying to smile at the skeptical person staring back at him. "I already answered any questions needing answers at the station. Would this be off the record?" "Scouts honor," musters Diaz, sticking his fingers up in promise.

Eli, amused with the officer's antics, sat at the nearby bench and gestured for the cop to sit and ask what he needed before his next class began. "You're not good at this. I thought detectives knew how to question people. You have fewer skills than that old guy back at the station."

"Ouch. Didn't think Lewis was more in touch with the youth than me. Anyway, when your next class is over meet me at that cafe. The Olive Branch." Diaz hands him his card and walks off, not giving Eli much of a choice but to oblige. This can't be that bad of an idea. Talking to the police. Off the record he says. Should I trust him Wis?

E sits at a vacant desk in his next class, blocking the interaction from his mind, forgetting it entirely as Daniel steals his pencil he was absentmindedly spinning.

—-

"Verdigris."

"I don't speak gibberish, Sir," Eli retorts, sliding into the booth, gesturing towards a waitress. "Hi ma'am. Can I have a hot chocolate, please?" After the charmed woman took his order, Elijah waited until she walked away before giving his attention to the inquisitive Detective.

"Hot cocoa?" mocks Matthew.

"Coffee stunts your growth, and matcha smells like grass. I mean, everyone knows that," he shrugs, before taking a sip of his newly arrived drink. What a weird guy, judging my tastes. "What's verdigris? Something that will tie me the murders?" Eli jokes downing the concoction in his cup. Diaz pointed to his lap."It's the stuff on your pants. Touch any pennies lately?" How did he know, what is this guy, psychic?

"I won't say, that's on a need-to-know basis. And you don't need to know." Eli quipped before changing the subject. "So what did you want to ask me about? Just the stains on my jeans?" "No. Now listen, this may seem far-fetched but everyone at the station thinks these killings are tied to you somehow. Not me though. I doubt Q is interested in some sarcastic teen. So following everyone's misguided delusions, I thought we could team up, on the record." Eli had no answers. This cop was loony.

How would he even know this. He just spoke to the police today so where was all of this info coming from. "Oh. And I know you and your friends were at the abandoned paint warehouse past curfew." Again, how does he know this? You're not ratting me out, are you, Wisdom?

"I am not confirming what you are saying is true, but what makes you think I want to work with you?" Diaz stares at the boy unamused. "I guess your parents would be happy to know you were digging around in an official police crime scene." Seriously, I am convinced you're cheating on me, Wis. How does this guy know this?

"Still not confirming anything, but go on." "Look, I'm not the type to go against protocol, but this killer is good. And every wise bone in my body is screaming to let you go and stick to my gut to crack this, but that would mean letting this case get cold. As much as I am a last resort in this mystery, I have come to the conclusion that so are you."

Eli's smile drops, not liking what this Detective is implying. "You have been in the vicinity of these murders roughly four times, considering the stuff on your pants isn't a coincidence. And to say the least, kid, you've got something." Eli nervously clears his throat. "I've got a death wish. That's what you are insinuating. Even if I thought what you were saying wasn't nuts, I still couldn't agree with your idea. Essentially, I would be used as bait."

What a psychotic idea. I can't do this. My Dad would kill me, heck, his lawyer would skin me for this impromptu conversation. Maybe I can make up some school related excuse and leave. But this guy seems too smart to fall for that. I mean, what would happen if I did go through with this? What if I take a chance with my mild case of plot armor and catch this psycho? Based on the trends, he doesn't seem to target males. Advantage Eli. But I can't. Am I really considering this?

I will regret this one day. Really regret this Wis.

Throughout all of this thinking, Diaz was still ranting on

about the benefits of them working together. The entire ordeal was overstimulating to Elijah.

"Stop," Eli stammers.

"You're right, what am I thinking? I am a detective, I could solve this on my own. I don't need the help of a kid fifteen years my junior." Diaz rambles while quickly sliding out of the booth, dropping a tip on the table. "Rude. You really need to work on your table manners." Elijah interjects. "I was just asking you to slow down, bro.

I'm in. What are we going to do?" No really. Wisdom, what are we going to do?

Permission

"Alright, I'm sorry. I know I should have listened to you and gone to the library. But how could I know there was any harm in going to the beach?" Eli pleaded in the plush passenger side of his Dad's car. "What did we say about shortcuts Elijah?" His Dad angrily musters. "Is this how you are always going to take things in life? So unseriously? I am angry, but it is because your Mom and I just want you to be safe, unlike the situation you could have been in."

Mr. Elliot slowed down at the red light. Sighing before turning his head to his son in the car. "You don't make it easy for me or your mother if we know you encounter crime scenes frequently. Really Elijah, what were you even doing on that side of town?" Eli sat quietly, allowing his Dad to continue. "Good thing that my coworker called and told us you were snooping around that abandoned paint shop. How careless do you have to be?"

"Warehouse," Eli interjects. "Plus I didn't know you were one to associate with snitches Dad. Not cool."

His Dad stills as the light turns green, looking at the foolish young man in front of him before continuing down the road. "That's strike one. Watch it, young man. When your mom hears about this, I know she will be disappointed. You can't joke your way out of our support and advice." Eli straightens up, realizing that his Dad is serious. "Not only that but let's not forget about that stunt you pulled at school, let's be real Elijah, your track record is untrustworthy." His Dad was referring to the call his professor gave him when Eli skipped a lecture to go to a concert in the neighboring town. Most professors don't care if you miss a class. But Eli was a top student and his reputation was proceeding him in all aspects of life.

"Okay, You're right. I haven't done my best to show you can trust me. And I know I could be in so much danger and I am glad you were there when I called. To be honest Dad, I thought it was a freaky art exhibit, who knew some lady died there in the sand."

"Hey, respect the dead, when you are talking. That could have been you, you know. Let's not go speaking down on the deceased." Mr. Elliot shakes his head, unimpressed by the excuses being uttered by his son. The streetlights shine again the windshield, as the car softly purrs in the rain. They continue the ride in silence, both convinced that the other was out of touch, unrelatable. So close yet so far away.

—-

What a dumb idea. I am going to die and I will have no one to speak on my true nature in my last moments, Eli thought. Will you write my eulogy? Looking bewildered at the detective in front of him, E wonders if it is too late to mark this as a fever dream and walk away with no scratches.

"That is the dumbest thing I ever heard. How will we even know that he will be there? Also what if he doesn't comply and now we all die because he knows of our plan?" Diaz turns to him, taking a breath before divulging the plan once more. "You think I'm far-fetched but how can I be crazy, when that is the energy we need to match? How do you know it will not work?"

Eli stares at the man imagining worms coming out of his ears. I am with a psycho, Wis. What am I going to do? Hope will kill me. Hell, Daniel will kill me. "Let me understand this. You're telling me that you want me to endanger one of my best friends because she seems to fit the bill as a target. Not only were you borderline stalking me to know I have a female friend, But you want me to use her as bait. And poof we catch the killer?" Diaz nods in confirmation.

Eli throws his hands up in disagreement, rushing towards the door to grab his things, but Diaz hurriedly beats him to the punch. "No. Well yes, but no." Diaz stammers. "This killer is different. He knows my mind and I his. There's a connection to say the least. Anyway, If I present him with a gift, he would mostly be intrigued and likely to oblige to my offer."

"Great I get paired up with a cop who thinks like a killer. Why not take me out now before I hand myself or my friends over on a silver platter?" Eli argues. "What even is the harm Elijah? If he doesn't take the bait there will be too many cops in the area for him to get away. Your friend Hope will be in no danger."

"No harm? Why can't you use some undercover cop lady? Also, it's Eli to you, only my parents use my government name," Eli states unamused at the offer being proposed. "Alright Eli. Come on, don't you want the people to know who this menace is, see you as the hero you are meant to be?"

"No." E declares. "I don't care about fame if my life is at stake. Legends are legends because they are dead. I don't need that title, I like my life. I'm a little shocked at how little you value them, Detective. Aren't you in the industry of saving people?"

"Alright, that's a bit below the belt Eli," Campbell interjects. "I think what Matthew here was trying to say is that you are not being presented as bait. We have been eyeing the clues and it looks like the killer operates strictly downtown. Where he disposes of most of the bodies we don't know."

"You haven't even found the bodies!?" I can't be the only smart one here. "I had little hopes before, but now I have heard enough. I'm done. See you detectives. Good luck with your search." E grabs the door handle already with the gall to walk out.

"Don't you think he knows?" Diaz whispers in a hushed tone. "He is coming for you anyway!" This stops Eli in his tracks. "Huh?" "You know, the killer." Diaz exclaims. "He can't be so naive to not know you were near almost four of the crime scenes. If we can connect the dots he probably already has plans for you. I guess we won't find your body as well since we are so incompetent. Right, Campbell?" Campbell nods in agreement, playing along with Diaz's attempts.

"That's not funny, and it won't work. The killer only wants girls, remember?" Eli stutters. "Is that what you believe? He has a way longer track record undisclosed, guys, girls, babies even." He's lying Wis, he has to be.

"I'm lying. Of course, he only goes after women, right Campbell?" Diaz laughs out. "I don't know, there was that one body," Campbell adds. "All that was left was the teeth. Male teeth according to the dental records. And that guy didn't even seem to witness anything. Seems like you're in more danger than him E."

Not falling for it. Nope. Should I? No. No. Maybe? But I am dumb, a huge idiot really, for falling for this. But what if, Wisdom? "Fine. I'm in. No more talk about teeth though. How freaky." The detectives high-five each other confident of their plan moving in action. "You won't regret this Eli, I know it," Diaz chimes.

Liars. I know I will Wis, pray for me.

—-

"I should kill you!" Daniel charges around the desk grabbing at Eli, but he dips backwards before falling over a chair. "Let me have him next!" Yells Hope in the opposite direction. "Hey, they promised you would be safe. C'mon guys!" "I expected this stupidity from Daniel," screams Hope.

"Hey! I'm not that dumb." Eli can't help but laugh. Even when his friends are angry they can still get a chuckle out of him.

"Hope you got it all wrong. The killer will not be there. They will just have you wired with a tracking device, while you are looking to see if there is anything suspicious in the area." Eli, out of energy from running, puts his hands up in surrender. Daniel grabs him by the shirt, looking at Hope for confirmation. "Fine," Hope says before smacking E on the shoulder. "If I die, I will come back and haunt you, you have my word."

"Thank you for that, but it will all be fine. Smooth sailing," Eli says, not sure if he is convincing her or himself anymore. Smooth sailing on rough waters indeed.

Caught

I know you've missed me. What? Surprised I'm still on the loose? I told you Wisdom. I am too good for this game, too smart for our petty police to catch. I implore you to take off the rose-colored glasses, and realize that most crimes go unnoticed and unattended. Now, I will give them some credit, the idea was peachy. Let's catch Mr. Q., bait him with a delectably fleshly Damsel, and I would be theirs. Trapped.

But my dearest Wisdom. Oh dearest friend. The police are pigs. I despise how they think I will eat the slop from their fat fingers. I am too luxurious for such disrespect. I mean I wouldn't call myself a serial killer, because the word is simply untrue. Or maybe it isn't. I'm a liar. Yet, I am consistent. And I have proved that this story won't end with me getting caught. That would send rather mixed signals to my fans.

So, to show my dedication to ever-changing games, I indulged them, edged them, and got away scot-free. I did receive a little help, though. Care to take a guess? Oh Wisdom. I wonder if this is cheating? Oh well, if it is, then lock me up then, and throw away the key.

Ha.

—-

"If this fails and I die, I will kill you, Eli," whispers Hope into the earpiece often donned by the Detectives. "How would that even work? I mean, you would be dead after all." Eli debates via walkie-talkie.

"Alright, that's enough you two, let's get in position," interjects Diaz into his receiver. "Now, I have my men around various locations to step in if anything suspicious happens. Hope, follow the path, and keep a watch out for anything weird. Tell us if you feel someone following you."

Hope nodded and started her walk. She stepped on Thirty-seventh Street and crossed the road amidst the traffic in an attempt to weave any possible suspect trailing behind her. Constantly being informed by dispatch on the direction to go next, she took the famous alleyway that plagued the city. An indication of the Damsel Eli had encountered. The shortcut that pulled them all into this game.

—-

"I was a witness to murder, and the police need my help." Eli dauntingly spoke to his friends the day before. "And you kept us in the dark for so long. Not cool bro. I thought we meant more to you." Ejected Daniel. "Okay, I have two questions. When was this? And what do the cops want you to help with?" Chimed Hope.

"Well about that, it's not just me. They need your help too," Eli muttered, rubbing the back of his neck.

—-

Even with the look she saw on Eli's face, if someone a week ago would've bet Hope all her money that she was going to be dragged into steering a police investigation, she would have lost everything she owned.

"I'm too good of a friend to you." She added to ease her nerves.

50

"You know, I should have let Daniel hit you more." Not caring much if E was even still on the other line. "Don't worry. I will get you back home safe in no time and we will get older and I will grow to be the best man at you two's wedding. Okay?" E thankfully replied.

"Nope. Uh-uh, you lost your spot, heck, you might not even get an invite at this point," she joked, trying to take the edge off of the situation before turning the corner and looking at the boats docked at the harbor.

"You don't have any other friends, sorry you are stuck with me," E replied. " That's not true I have plenty of friends ready to replace you at a moment's notice," she playfully said, happy that Eli was allowed to talk her through this. In her peripheral view she saw another cop in hiding, before walking onto another busy road.

Relieved that the walk was almost over, she sauntered towards a van, elated that she was close to her destination. Eli stood beside her as she took all the police gear off. "I guess we didn't catch him," he muttered. "Welp. Good luck with your endeavor Detectives, please never call us again."

"Woah, woah, woah. Slow down Eli, we will pick this up tomorrow," Campbell interrupted. "Hope, darling, be here at seven a.m., we will try to do it in the morning to rule out possible time-related M.O.s."

"I usually don't even have class that early, but sure, whatever helps the case right?" Hope added, looking towards Eli disappointingly. "Whatever helps the case," Eli replied, trying to reassure his friend.

As Hope approached toward the agreed spot the next day, she sat on the curb angsty with how early she had to get there. Annoyed to find that she was the first to arrive. "Where are you,

E?" She shivered into her phone. "Almost there. I am down the block. Diaz is with me, hold on." Eli couldn't believe he overslept. Then there was traffic on the bus. His morning was full of mishaps so hopefully this day would be better.

"Did you hear me? Hope, hello?" Eli asked, shocked there was no witty answer in response to his lateness.

"She heard you just fine Elijah, just fine. Thank you for the rose," the cryptic man, now sporting magenta sunglasses, spat into the phone, before hanging up.

The blood drained from Eli's face as he rushed to the spot with Diaz, only seeing Hope's phone and a black envelope where she should have stood.

"I'm sorry E, we will find her," spoke Diaz. Eli slumped to the ground in fear, too shaken with the idea that his friend was gone and could be dead in the next moments. He failed to register any of the words Diaz said, steadily thinking of one thought. Daniel is going to kill me. Wisdom could you kill me first?

—-

Dear Mr. Elliot,
& Mr. Diaz, since he is probably reading this too.
Hell. Hi Campbell.

I know you are surprised. You should be. I beat you and I additionally received a glorious flower to add to my collection. I didn't realize how much you guys knew me. How sweet. I always thought red was too strong, but pink. Pink is perfect.

Thank you. You did the hard part for me.

Watching you guys yesterday in all those rosy efforts, without reaching out to grab her was hard. Tempting even. What great feelings you have brought back to me. I was beginning to feel bored.

But this is giving me a rush of euphoria!

Now don't despair, Elijah, you're young so I can excuse your naivety. Stay in school kid, you need it. But those two imbeciles, reading along, they deserve to be punished. Dragging a poor prize around the city. Don't you know there are serial killers in the area? How foolish.

I know you have questions and thankfully for you, I have offered solutions. Below I will display almost an address of where little Hope is left. Get it? Little Hope? I am hilarious. Anyway I digress. Under this paper is another. That is the clue. A clue on how to find this rose, for one is all you will get.

I know, cryptic. I mean how can you trust that I am where I imply to be? You can't. But you really have no option but to do the one thing that goes against your heart, your genetic makeup. Trusting that little voice in your head that is similar to me.

So choose wisely, try your best, or give up on Hope. I win either way. Here's to you. Finding, that you are less, very little, but no different to me.

Undoubtedly,
  Mr. Q.

P.S.
  You suck at this game Diaz, how about next round you bring the heat. That's all you're good for anyway. Burning bridges.

Elijah stood up from his chair pushing Diaz and Campbell out of the way, exiting toward the hall, contemplating if he should mention any of this to his parents. Daniel was sitting near the lobby, refusing to talk to him, before giving up on the notion, rising from his seat in a rush of anger. "I told you she was in danger, Eli why can't you stop dragging us into your messes!?" Daniel shouted. "If she dies I will never forgive you. You hear me. If Hope is gone, we are done."

Elijah stared at the floor. I won't forgive myself, he thought. I need serious help.

Can you help me, Wisdom? Please?

Honey

"That's all you're good for anyway. Burning bridges."

Diaz was stuck. The Captain warned him that if he didn't find Hope within the next 10 hours, he would be off the case, facing suspension, and possible legal issues with Eli's parents for endangering him and his friends during a time of distress. That was 8 hours ago, and despite the brain-racking, he was still stuck.

But why did those specific words stick to him? Like a cancer within himself, he began to believe them. I burn everything I touch. I could do better if I handed in the badge; it would at least do these women good, rather than being burned.

Burned bridges.
Burned.
Bridges.

That's it, he thought, running to Campbell asking to see the letter for the eighty-seventh time. As grabbed the paper, he began to circle various phrases that stood out to him.

"Under this paper is another. That is the clue. A clue on how to find this rose, for one is all you will get.

How about next round, you bring the heat. That's all you're good for anyway. Burning bridges."

"Campbell, look!" He turned toward his tired partner. These words. "Under, clue, rose, one, round, for, bridge." Campbell stared at him in confusion. "Huh? Can you make sense, please? I think you finally lost it." Diaz shook his head and pointed at the paper again. "He gave us the map right here! It reads like this.

Underneath is the clue to find the rose, one round about the fourth bridge.

He jolted with newfound energy and pulled up his radio from his holster, informing dispatch to give out the address to any of the other police officers, calling for everyone in the vicinity. "Unit Seven, please respond to under the Roundabout Bridge on Fourteenth Street for a missing persons. One Hope Andrews, female, Asian, age nineteen. Call it in and advise on arrival."

"Copy that dispatch, Unit Seven, responding to under the Roundabout Bridge on Fourteenth Street for missing persons," an officer reiterates. Diaz hoped he wasn't on the wrong track, but this was a chance. A chance close to saving this girl who did nothing but trust him. This would be the first victim, he could save since these killings began.

"Matt!" Campbell snaps him out of his thoughts, telling him to hurry along. In a rush, he grabs his gun, his badge, and the letter before heading off.

—-

"Did they say anything? It's been almost half a day." Daniel asked while pacing across Eli's living room. The police sent the both of them home around the fifth hour when no answers were found. "E, I can't lose her, then I will be stuck with you,

56

and right now I want to hit you. What do you think will happen if we're all that's left?" mutters Daniel before flopping on the couch.

"If they can't find her, then we will. It's as simple as that." Eli retorted. "You can wail on me all you want we we get her home. Deal?" Eli followed suit and began to pace the floor, thinking about the letter he read. The cops took it for evidence, of course, but before they got their grubby hands on it, he took a screenshot. The silence from the police was deafening and Eli was racking his mind for answers.

"What are you two plotting? Stay put until they call," Eli's mom yells from the kitchen. "Alright, Mom. Daniel and I are listening, we just need to go down the hall to his house, and check if his parents heard anything."

He tapped Daniel on the shoulder and walked out the apartment door, before his mom could protest.

Outside in the hall, he looked at Daniel, who was looking at him quizzically for instructions. A light bulb went off in his head as he headed for the stairway. One thing he knew was that the cops were undependable until it was too late.

"Daniel, let's go, I have a hunch," he spoke as they winded down the staircase and headed towards the block. Forget what everyone is saying Wisdom. I have to save my friend. Right now, you can be wise for the both of us.

Within the cop car, Diaz was trying to let Campbell into his thought process on how he knew where the location of the hostage was, before looking out the window. As he spoke, he saw Daniel and Eli running in the same direction they were going along the sidewalk.

"Where are you guys headed?" he yelled out the window.

"Fourteenth Bridge, you?" Shouts Eli. "Same, hop in." The car slowed to a stop allowing the duo to join the older in the car. Once they filed in, Campbell hit the gas pedal to make up for lost time.

"So how'd you guys come to the same conclusion like we did?" The Lieutenant asks, impressed with Elijah. "Well, within the letter, I'm barely mentioned, which is weird, even though Hope is my friend. I figured it had to be directed toward Diaz. Which then made me stare more at it for some hidden meaning. With that, the word bridges stood out. Then we went from there."

"We could use a kid like you on the force." Eli shook his head defiantly. "No, if Diaz is getting heat like this from some killer, I wouldn't be surprised if I made even more enemies." Daniel laughed beside him. "Yeah. That's because you have a big mouth. You don't know when to stop," he interjected, earning a shove from Eli. Elijah sulked, disrupting the flow of the conversation, before the silence ate at him, forcing him to turns toward Diaz quietly.

"Do you still have the letter on you, both pages?" "Yeah, why?" questioned the detective. "No reason." I hope. Wis, I said I had a hunch.

—-

The scene at the bridge was a beehive. The news, the bridge, the cops, and the civilians. All buzzing. Diaz and Campbell told Eli and Daniel to stay safe behind the police tape near the Captain in case they were needed.

"Eli, I know your folks don't know you are here. Don't be a hero. Because I can't face your parents with news of your death if things go wrong, okay?" Diaz urged the young man, staring him in the eye as if his breaking that promise would crumble what little hope Diaz had in this whole thing going right.

"Yeah, yeah, I got it. Go save Hope, stop worrying about me." Eli said before pushing the Detective towards their friend. Hope was under the bridge, screaming for help. Her voice was coarse from the prolonged crying. Tears rolling down her face, as she trembled from the pain of a knife being held harshly into her cheek.

Diaz froze, staring at the spectacle before him, afraid that if he reached out toward her, something bad would happen. As he approached slower, he spoke cautiously. "Hope, we're here. We will get you out of here; just tell us what's going on."

"I can't. He told me that you have to be smarter than that, Detective!" She whisper-yells at him. "Okay, okay, take it easy." Diaz inches closer, before a figure hops up near her body, grabbing at the knife and pulling it out of her face. Hope cries in pain, begging the cops to stay back. Bewilderment hit their faces, all of the officers kept their guns facing the standing body, with the figure wielding the knife back at them.

"Don't shoot, don't shoot," begs Hope. "You don't understand, you don't get it! Please don't shoot," she says before fully breaking down into a hysterical sob. An officer on the side slowly steps into the frame, grabbing at Hope. It was the same one who helped interrogate Eli with Lewis.

The figure hopped into defense and lunged at the officer, stabbing him in the process. This series of events unfolded with all of the surrounding police shooting at them. Hope screamed out once more, half-shocked by the slurry of bullets and half-terrified of the consequences that would come as a result of that police officers' actions.

Diaz leaped forward and grabbed Hope, backing away from the body still on the ground. Hope squirmed out of his arms and yelled at everyone in the vicinity. "What is wrong with you all!? Can't you use you're heads? Look at them!" She pointed to the lifeless body, while another cop uncovered their face slowly, showing that it was a woman; a victim as well, on the floor bleeding into the pavement, soul slipping rapidly.

Eli lowered his head, blaming himself for putting everyone in danger. If he never agreed to Diaz's request then none of this would have happened. While the thoughts in his head were clouding his judgment, Daniel began running towards Hope. As he reached out for her, Campbell yelled for everyone to back away. "Diaz, something's not right. Do you hear that?" Hope backed up from the crowd, more-so trying to distance herself while reaching for the device stuck to her back.

It was ticking.

"Hope stay calm, but I think you have a bomb on your back," yelled Eli. She shot him a panicked face laced with hints of bewilderment, as to how clueless he thought she was towards the situation she was in. Eli ran towards Diaz, confusing the girl even more with his antics.

"Matt. Do you trust me?" asked E.

"Not really. Hey, what did I say about staying out of the way?"

"Come on, I have an idea." he pleaded. "That's what I'm afraid of," he uttered, still obliging to hearing him out, as Eli leaned closer to let him in on his plan. As Elijah finished his thoughts, Diaz nodded in understanding, took out a pen, and wrote something down. Then he ran quickly and threw the paper on the chair that Hope was tied to. Just as Elijah suspected, the countdown of the weapon on his friend's back had slowed to a stop.

Like I said, Wis, the cops are really useless.

Withered

"It wasn't dark, not like how the movies make you think. The room we were in was very bright, with colors splashed everywhere, almost innocent-looking, under different circumstances. However, there were no windows but the ones self-painted, almost child-like."

Hope trembled in remembrance, trying to recall everything that occurred within the last few days. Clearly shook from the traumatic experience.

"Please continue," urged one of the therapists assigned to help in these kinds of situations. "Right. Sorry." She sighed with a shaky breath. "It was all a blur. When I first got taken, I didn't even get knocked out, just blindfolded. The ride was smooth, and despite my yelling and protesting, I almost felt like an accomplice or a guest rather than a victim." The therapist nodded, scribbling into a notebook paying no mind to the sadness lacing Hope's words. After a few seconds she looked up and gestured for her to continue.

"I can't speak for the other woman, though. She was treated far worse than I was, and ended up dying when I can confirm she did nothing wrong."

The therapist sighed and then opened her mouth. "Are you sure about that Hope? She held a knife to your face and stabbed an officer. I wouldn't say they didn't do something wrong."

Our four heroes stood outside the two-way mirror, silently listening to everything being said. "I could kill him," muttered Daniel. "Same, it's personal now." Agreed Eli, staring at Hope, guilt getting to him as he eyed her sunken face and bloodshot eyes.

"Shh, you two, we need to hear this for the record. I still have a lot to explain to the Captain, and it would be best if I could hear," spoke Campbell before turning his attention back to the session.

"You wouldn't understand. He was weird in the way he treated us. He referred to me as a flower. Like I was a guest, even though I don't know why he kept going on and on about roses. But he called the other woman Wisdom. It was freaky, like he was talking beyond her, instead of to her." She closed her eyes picturing the situation, trying to make reason with a killer's antics. "I know people can do that sometimes, get distracted with what's in their heads, and dissociate, like my friend Eli does, but this was something different. Eerie."

Eli straightened with the realization that others could feel him blanking, which of course didn't go unnoticed by Diaz, who kept quiet amidst the mini conversations breaking out.

Taking another breath, Hope touched her bandaged face. "He's sick, you won't catch him. I was there, and even with his attention on the other woman, I didn't think I would make it out of there for a second. He was meticulous in every movement. Voice changer, ropes, and weapons from what I could see. He even had a large supply of paper; fancy stationery."

"Okay, well, him being caught will depend on the investigation and the police. No killer gets away fully." The woman chimed in. Therapists always think they know more than you. How is that even possible? Wis, they hear our side of things for the very first time, while we are reliving the moments experienced. If anything, they are the ones out of the loop and behind.

"He isn't just some killer. That's where you are wrong. He was despicable, like we were appetizers to a bigger meal. I wasn't even harmed by him. Not directly." "Go on," spoke the therapist, intrigued. "He scarred that woman. Turned her against me. He told her that if she harmed me, he would eventually let her go. She had no choice, and I don't blame her because she's gone now, but look at me!"

Hope yelled at the woman scribbling on paper. "I was kidnapped, mentally tortured like a pawn in a chess game, held under a bridge for hours, stabbed, and then I had a bomb strapped to my back." She yelled pointing at her fingers in anger and fear.

"That woman, whose face I didn't know and can't remember, got treated far worse than me. You are not listening," she scoffed. "Do you get it? She was his real victim and no one even knew she was missing." Hope was trembling by this point. "He's always ten steps ahead and we are so behind it feels like a completely different game."

Daniel was seething, fed up with the constant back and forth. He walked out of the room and opened the door to the other side. "That's enough! Don't you know you're scaring her, lady?" He shouted at the shocked therapist. Eli ran to grab him, with Campbell following after. Diaz ignored the rising argument and continued to look at Hope, surprised to see her stand up.

"No! Look at me," pulling off her bandage. "This is beyond us, if we keep digging, he will keep killing, look at what he made her do to my face!"

64

—-

I am no monster. I am getting tired of having to remind you of that Wisdom. "I am too nice to cut a poor Damsel with a kitchen tool. So you," pointing to the other victim, instructing her to walk towards Hope.

Hope was confused. If this woman was untied, why didn't she stop him or run away? She just moved like slow water inching closer and closer towards her. She was registering how much danger she was in and began pleading for the woman to stay away. "I don't get it. Why are you doing this?" Mr. Q. chuckled.

"Drugs. I get that you are confused, dear Hope, but she is drugged. It's a mix of a lot of things, essentially turning her mind into putty. I also added a few drops of LSD for good measure." He turned to look around the room before settling on a simple knife on the table.

"Oh. I'm silly." He smiled. "Was that question directed at me? Well, I do it for fun, lovely Hope. Art is often lost on the crowd. Ask anyone," snickering, "Sorry, I guess you can't do that since you are preoccupied, silly me." The man eased beside the standing Damsel, holding her hand tightly so that her grip clasped around the knife centimeters from Hope's face.

Hope screamed a guttural sound, as the knife led by Mr. Q's instruction carved intricately into the side of her face like a canvas, creating a bloodied rose image. The woman, although delirious, cried from the noise, not fully registering her actions within it all, but reacting to Hope's cries and pain nonetheless.

"Uh-oh. Let's dry those tears my rose, for the fun is just beginning," mocked Mr. Q before throwing the drugged woman to the ground and wiping Hope's blood from the knife. "Don't worry. I am not going to kill you two. Knowing the cops they will do the easy part for me."

—-

It's not that bad really. Think of it as kind of like a tattoo. Only indented," chimed Daniel, trying to ease the situation the best he could. Hope turned to him, shocked, while Eli smacked the back of his head in annoyance. "Dude, not helping. She doesn't have to like it." "Sorry," mumbled Daniel.

Eli replied turning towards his friends. "No Daniel. It's my fault. Guys, I'm sorry for dragging us into this. I truly thought you would be safe Hope. I would have never expected this to happen." "It's okay, E. I am alive, aren't I?" Hope whispered sympathetically. "Yeah, water under the bridge," added Daniel, holding onto her hand. "Sorry, too soon." She shook her head before laughing

I'd laugh too if I didn't feel so guilty.

"Hey E, since we're still on the topic, how did you know how to stop the bomb?" Inquires Hope. "I didn't know. Not really. I just thought that it was weird that the killer had sent a letter and a piece of paper with no words on it." Eli shrugged his shoulder and stood up. They all walked to his room down the hall. After they hurriedly sat on his bed, he softly closed his door before whispering to his friends in a hushed tone.

"At the station, I considered writing him back, but then I thought it was dumb since I don't know where to send it to. That's why I asked Diaz in the car if he took the letter. Even then, I didn't know he had the extra sheet or a pen too." "Man, talk about quick instincts," cheesed Daniel, getting up to tackle Eli in appreciation. As they joked around, Hope stared at the friend in front of her. An idea popping in her head.

"What if we try to do that? Send him letters, and mark the

locations of where he picks them up. Like a locator of sorts, narrow down the search?" "I think we should give it a rest, try to move past serial killers," Eli stated. "Yeah, what are the odds we'll catch him anyway? I should try to just get used to not being a hostage," agreed Hope.

It's actually a great idea, Wis. What would I even say to Q if the opportunity arose. We know you are looking for us, so here lets become writing buddies? I need help. A few hours later when his friend left for their homes, he texted Diaz of the idea.

Hey Diaz. I won't endanger my friends anymore. If this plan goes into motion, it will have to be just me and you. Not even Campbell can know. Deal? – E.

How did you even get this number? But okay, I agree. I will meet you at our spot and go over the clues we do have. See you soon.
- Detective Diaz.

Pen Pals

To the Dearest Diaz & Evident Elijah,

I am shocked you caught on to what I was intending. Point Elijah! I know Diaz had no mind for it, he can be quite dim at times. Pity on your end I guess. It was cute, seeing you all scramble, as the time on Hope's back dwindled. Yes, I was there. Watching. Surprised?

You really shouldn't be, I do implore that you do not react so hastily to everything I do, heart problems occur in those easily frightened. I am getting off-topic. I thought your letter was rather rushed.

"I see you. Both players in this game. May the best man win."- Diaz

See, it is rather dry. Do better next time, or I might have to punish you for such efforts. Consequently, I will give you a penalty now because I wanted this game to be just between us. You see, I am the jealous type and I don't like to share, so Elijah, thank the next victim on you. I will drag her just as you dragged yourself into this game.

It's too late for regrets.

Unamused,
  Mr. Q.

P.S.
  Elijah. I see you are similar to me. Have you spoken to Wisdom lately? Seems they are playing on both sides. Reminds you of anyone?
  —-

Yikes. "You never told me his letters were so creepy," Eli exclaimed, shivering from the language on the paper. "That's what you got from that? He just said that there will be another victim and that you guys have something in common. What's up with that?" Diaz shouts bewildered at Eli's apathy.

"You believe him? He could be bluffing. Also, if there is a victim, we could just find them first. Don't we have the police on our side?" Eli questions. "One, this is off the record unless Captain can give me a special team for this type of stuff. Two, this killer is weird and knows too much, but he isn't a liar. Someone will die because of this. Three, you never answered my other question." Eli turns to the Detective, not sure of what to do next.

I'm wondering that too. You really are cheating on me. I thought you were only my friend, Wis? Should I tell him, he would probably think I'm crazy. Even though it seems you've betrayed me, Wisdom, what should I do? "Fine, I'll tell you what's up with me when you tell me what Q has on you, and why you are so involved in this in the first place." Diaz goes silent. "That's none of your business." "Then it's none of your business either." Eli retorts. They sit in silence for a while longer until Campbell walks in with drinks in his hand.

"I thought we agreed it was just us?" Eli mutters. "I thought you were joking. We need him. Campbell is good at finding the locations and origins of the weapons and substances used in the murders. The man has connections. I will focus on finding the victims and sorting through the clues. And you. You will be writing the letters since your friend "Q" has a soft spot for you." I'm on homework duty? Great.

"Why does it seem that I am getting the short end of the stick?" Eli says, slumping into his chair."That's because you are. I need to keep an eye on you. If your parents knew what you were doing, they would kill me. Sue the station, and then kill you." "Right. Guess I'll stick to the homework. Do we at least know where to drop the letters off to? He sends them to us, but where do we get them to him?"

"Well, I have an idea for that," interjects Campbell. "He wouldn't want to get caught, obviously, and based on that letter he wrote to us about your friend Hope, he most likely gave us the address for the next pick-up within this letter." "So he is running the scavenger hunt. How do we get him to play our game?" asks E.

"That's where I come in," says Diaz. "He wants me. So to get him out of his comfort zone, I will find the victims first and drop off the letters. We have to stop him before he can act. I am working with other agencies to see if there are any clues to his motives. I want you to do the same, so get to writing, it's almost go time." I guess this is a plan of sorts. I mean, how bad can this really get?

—-

To Q.,

Excuse the grammar issues, because most of my generation works digitally, so this is very old school in my opinion.

Diaz and Campbell say hi. So there's that. I don't have big words or some cryptic message, at least not for this first letter. I just want to give you a warning.

I will find you. My family are my non-negotiables, and you crossed the line. See Hope, she is forgiving, and Daniel is like our glue. But me. I have something you don't. I hear it all. I see from the outside. And there are holes in your story. You lack something, and when I find out what that is, I will send my people to do my dealing.

Because, like I said, I have something you don't. Friends, support, ask Wisdom. See if they speak back to you. On the plus side, I doubt you would really kill a woman for my sake. Because if you do that it means I'm important. More important than you.

Geez. I guess anyone can stoop low to give out threats. I really don't like being the center of attention. Anyway, like I said, Diaz says hello and that you will soon meet "Rain", whatever that means.

Unafraid,
  Eli

P.S.
   Those who write P.S. notes are lazy. If you couldn't get your words out right, you should have written a new letter. Or is this game truly not that important to you? Is paper too expensive? Get your priorities straight, man. You're confusing even me.

"I don't know about this guys. What if he takes me up on my offer and actually kills some poor lady?" Eli wonders. "He can't, that means you win, it would be too easy now. So I think we just bought ourselves some time. Good work, E. Even I feel threatened by this," chimes Campbell. "Let's just see how this goes. So what's next?"

"Now it's time to catch this guy." Let the games begin.

Monochromatic

He took me up on my offer, Wisdom. "Think it was wise to threaten a madman, Diaz?" Eli prodded with a face that spelled 'I told you so.' "Despite what you're thinking," stated Diaz, "I already planned for this." "You mean I planned for this?" Campbell spoke, walking into the room.

"Remember how this guy never had a linking motive. Well, we still haven't found it, but something he does do is pride himself in being eccentric." Campbell rolled out the whiteboards and started scribbling words down. "I don't know why I got this hunch, but considering he kept killing women, and then a pregnant one to bait Diaz into joining his sick game, I thought it was due time that he would want something that repeated itself."

Eli sat up, he never knew Q. killed a pregnant woman. If he did then he would have been nicer in his first letter to him. Returning back to Campbell's remarks he got stuck on the word repeating. It can't, he thought. Q. couldn't have.

"You don't mean-" He shrieked.

"Yes. Triplets." Campbell spoke.

Diaz watched as Eli pulled out a piece of paper and began writing. "I thought you had writer's block?" "Detective, I thought of all people, you would understand that inspiration can stem from anywhere?" Diaz continued to prod, "Is that what Wisdom said to you? Again, who is that?"

Eli froze and then continued to write. I am going to ignore that for now. He is just fishing for anything at this point. I doubt the killer really talks to you, Wis. I doubt Diaz has caught on either.

Right?

Diaz laughed at how serious E had become in the past few days. Proud in a sense, as well, that he was becoming more mature. Even though it required searching for a serial killer in order to catapult him into character development.

Campbell cleared his throat. "Anyway. Like I was saying, three sisters went missing yesterday. It was called in from the neighboring state since the last anyone had heard of them was when they arrived at the Heartland Airport at eight-fifteen last night."

Eli shivered at the thought that Q. would be scouting airports for potential victims. No one is safe in this town until we catch him. Will you help me? Wisdom, I'm not mad at you anymore. I don't think I ever was.

"Any idea where he might have taken them?" Diaz proposed. "Yes, that's where you come in, Matt. The TSA has a few clues, including images of the three suspects, which puts us at an advantage since usually there is no description of what the victims look like." "And what about me?" interjected Eli

"You, my friend, will need a really good letter. Get writing." Great, more homework. Diaz and Campbell both looked at how dejected Eli became, and broke, laughing at the younger counterpart. "I don't get what's so funny." Eli pouted.

"Write your letter, then come on!" They smiled. "You mean I get to come along? Alright! Let me call my house and tell my mom I will be late for dinner. Thanks, guys!" Eli rang his house phone. No answer, just a voicemail. I forgot. Mom's at Daniel's, helping his older sister bake. Oh well. He grabbed his stuff and ran out the door towards the police car.

—-

"Dispatch said they got a description that matched the three girls." "That was a bit fast, guess this guy is getting sloppy," spoke Diaz with surprise. We might actually catch him, Eli thought. As he sat in the back of the cop car, writing the last of his letter, he couldn't help but focus on the fact that it had been six days since the one he received from Mr. Q. and it was shocking how for the past week, the streets felt safer.

Until now.

"We have to catch this guy," E urged. "This town was just starting to feel safer." "Don't go getting confused on me, Elijah, it will never be safe until we find him. Him being quiet now just means he was plotting something for longer. Luckily, he is greedy and decided to take three girls at once. But let's keep our guard up, okay?" Diaz pushed, hoping no one would get reckless before they found the kidnappees.

"We're here. Wherever here is." Campbell said, slowing the car to a stop. "Have you never been to a movie theater? Really how old are you?" joked Eli. "I am not that old. Look, this has nothing to do with age, I just don't get out much." muttered Campbell, defending himself.

"Is this place familiar to you, Eli? Why would the women be here?" Diaz asked, unbuckling his seat belt and closing the door behind him. "I used to go here with my friends. It's shut down now, but the last time I went was about five weeks ago when I..."

"When you what?"

"When I saw Q. drown the women in the alley." When we both saw her die, remember?

The dark and cramped alleyway where that kind Damsel fell to her demise. Searching for air above her grasp as he clenched and tore the life from her lungs until there were no more bubbles to breathe out. A night that pulled me into a sea of trouble. Wading and fighting against the current. Hoping it wouldn't drag me away.

"Well, there is no use getting spooked now. Let's go inside. E, you stay behind us in case this is a trap. If anything weird happens, phone for help." Diaz whispered. "Got it," agreed Eli, as the trio slowly approached the entrance. Opening the door, they walked inside, searching for any signs of something strange happening after hours.

"No one is supposed to be here this late, right?" asked Eli, frightened by the darkness they were witnessing. "Well, we got the call that they would be here, so I guess someone should be around. How about each of us start with a section of the theater and go to the various rooms? If you find them, call for us." Campbell commanded, handing Diaz and Eli walkie-talkies and flashlights.

Elijah grabbed the devices, took a deep breath, and started towards the section at the far end. I can do this, there is nothing creepy about being in an empty theater all alone, and the only people to depend on are Campbell and Diaz, who are an earshot away and will probably be late by the time they arrive anyway. Right, nothing to be worried about, at least I have you, Wis.

As he ducked in briefly into each room, boredom was seeping in, and he was beginning to think that there was nothing to be found. Then a poster across the hall from him started flickering with light. Strange, he thought, pulling out the walkie in case of any issues, and slowly entered into the theater. There was no indication that the women were there. So he turned to exit just the same.

But then a noise began on the projector screen. "Elijah. Eager Elijah. You are certainly very warm. Don't leave just yet. Sit and watch this short film I have constructed." The voice, unrecognizable to him, was a woman's. Which was strange, to say the least. Did Q. have a sidekick? Additionally, another woman chimed in, and then a third. "Please stay. Our lives depend on it." He was confused but amidst all of this, he held his hand on the talk button, hoping one of the detectives got the memo to come from the noise occurring.

How creepy, Wis. And this guy talks to you?

On the flickering screen, the three sisters were in a room full of film equipment, tied up with their arms behind themselves, mouths covered, but no real signs of a struggle. Maybe they were in on it? Can't be. They had to be drugged of some sort. Hearing them talk you could depict a slurring to their words. "Alright, Q., give it up," he shouted. "Just tell me where the women are and we can come to some kind of agreement. Preferably before anyone got hurt."

"You are rather impatient," another voice chimed in, this time a male's. "Don't be like Diaz, prioritizing the wrong thing. I thought your letter was cheeky, very brazen, I must say. However, I am super disappointed, Elijah, that you thought I wouldn't take you up on your offer. Don't belittle your importance. I warned you that if you dragged yourself further, I would do the same."

"You told me it would be just one victim, not three," Eli said, searching under chairs and shining his flashlight across the theater for clues. "Tsk. Tsk. You just don't get it. Those women are the same; they mimic each other's color, but you're right, I did promise just one so fine. Come get them."

The image of the women on the screen suddenly turned around and showed Eli's back. This caught his attention, and he knew to run to the projector room. Getting there in just a few steps he burst open the door. Eli saw the women and jumped to untie their restraints. Once they were loose, he called for Diaz and Campbell to come. As they ran in to help the hostages, a figure left out the emergency exit. Eli hearing the door, ran out the room and witnessed the killer's escape. Just as he began running down the stairs in pursuit to the theater, a voice on the screen abruptly stopped him. The images on the screen showing a ghastly figure.

"Elijah, what did I say about patience? I know your mother taught you better than that." The ominous voice echoed. "Why don't you come back, you coward, and face me like a real man?" He shouted back at the screen. "I would think that amidst all this trouble occurring you would phone home. I mean, I did promise you a victim of my dragging."

"What is he talking about?" Turned Diaz now beside him, staring at Eli's face, flushed of all its color. Elijah ignoring the detective, pulled out his phone and dialed the numbers of his house, hands shaking, hoping someone would pick up.

Ring. Ring. Ring.

No answer.

Ring. Ring. Ring.

No answer.

Ring. Ring. Ring.

Beep.

Elijah sighed in relief, slightly ashamed at how panicked he'd become. He put his phone on speaker before speaking. "Hello, Mom! Are you okay?" But there was no response. Nothing. Why don't I hear anything? "Hello!?" "Why hello, eager Elijah. This should come to no surprise. I mean I thought I made myself clear. One victim."

"We have your victims here Q.," yelled Diaz at the phone. "Oh hi detective. I am glad you are here but if I were you I would be quiet so I can continue talking to Elijah. I don't like being interrupted." Diaz closed his mouth, turning to look at Elijah who looked like he was a second from passing out.

The voice on the phone chuckled. "Anyway, can you hear that my friend?" "Hear what, you sicko? Where is my mother!?" "Shh. Listen, and you shall receive." Eli held his breath to focus on a rustling sound on the other end. "What are you doing to her!" He screamed helplessly.

"Me? I am dragging your mother away, like promised. I think it is best if you hurry, who knows? You might even catch us."

Click.

Glass

Elijah hopped out of the car and ran up the stairs, skipping a few with each step in a rush. As he got to his parents' apartment, he held his hand on the doorknob, scared to turn it and confirm what he already knew in his heart. She's gone, isn't she? And it's all my fault.

A figure touched him on the shoulder, causing his soul to jump out of his body momentarily. It was his Dad, unamused and back from a long shift. "Woah, why are you so jumpy?" He scanned Eli's face, suspicion washing over his own. "What is the problem? Dog got your tongue?"

"Dad, I have something to tell you." He opened the unlocked door and walked inside, revealing a mess of a living room. "Mom is gone." Eli lowered his head in shame, afraid to look at his Dad's face. "What do you mean, Elijah?" His voice filling with concern. "Did your mom see this mess?" He placed his things down and walked towards the kitchen table, picking up a black envelope in the process. "What is this, an invitation?"

"No, Dad! Mom got kidnapped." Elijah walked near his Dad and reached for the envelope in his hand. He put on the most serious face he could and opened his mouth once more confessing, "I went against your wishes and got involved in the investigation, and that psycho killer kidnapped Mom!"

His Dad let go of the envelope, eyes locked with his, half expecting this to be some joke, and pulled out his phone, dialing his wife. No answer. He dialed it once more, but again, no answer. Panicked, he started to dial the police. But before he could get the last number out, Eli stopped him, placing his hand over the phone.

"The police are here. I just need you to trust me." He urged. "That's just it Elijah, I don't. And when we get your mother back, and I mean when, we will discuss how to deal with you." Eli nodded and knelt to the ground beginning to pick up some of the mess. "That's fair Dad, but can Detective Diaz come in?" he gestured towards the door. His Dad agreed but stopped at the door telling him to leave the mess in case of clues.

Continuing, Mr. Elliot let the other officers in, including some of forensic scientists as he predicted, and they began searching the living room and kitchen. Before Diaz could enter fully, he punched him square in the jaw. "That is for endangering my wife and my son."

Police officers ran to stop him, but Diaz held his hand out, telling them to stop before speaking. "I understand, sir, but I advise we discuss this after we find Eli's mother. The kidnapper is the real issue here."

Not minding the commotion in the house, Eli opened the letter addressed to him as the living room became a blur of bodies.

Dear Elijah the enthusiastic,

This is a fumble of your own doing. I warned you. I really did.

I merely executed my word, which I gave truthfully. See I'm no monster, no liar. I do want to share this with you. Your mother makes magnificent cookies. So warm and delectable. Just like she was before I knocked her out, dragging her amongst the floor (to keep my promise of course), and stuffing her in my vehicle before driving to my unknown destination. Can you guess where I am? It's very clear to see.

I anticipate you will find her. And don't worry, I won't harm your precious mom. I just wanted to get a very clear message across to you.

That when you aim for the moon, you shall get scorched by the sun in the process.

Unimpressed,
  Mr. Q.

P.S.
  I am not lazy. I am simply an opportunist. You, my friend, could learn a few things about timing. Also, your mother is a fabulous baker. I might have to stop by more often.

Eli read the letter amidst the riot occurring in his house. He scanned and searched until Diaz had to grab him by the shoulders, and urge him to look up. "We'll find her, and know that it's not your fault; anyone can see that clear as day. Okay?" Eli nodded solemnly not fully believing the detective but being grateful that he was here. "Pass the letter here, let's see if I can help."

"That's alright. I solved the letter. I just don't know if I should tell everyone, though. Someone here is untrustworthy, like, how did he even get my address? I'll show you because you asked, but that's it. We can't have this thing leaked, and she ends up dying for it."

—-

How peculiar.

She is something, to say the least. Turning the corners as if a circle was her destination. You know, I often ignore the colors around me, but I never thought to see someone so plain in my sight. It's almost endearing. I wonder if she knows how special she is.

Is it crazy to follow her across town? I mean, I don't do this kind of thing ever. It is rather unbecoming and unlike me to succumb to my instincts and follow someone, anyone, around. To match the pace of her walking and duck out of her peripheral vision like a shadow, is quite exhilarating.

Am I a stalker? A watcher of women? I guess now I am. Is it wrong that it feels like second nature? Maybe saying it out loud is wrong. She is quite nimble, ducking corners and checking her surroundings. Would it be strange if I just took her? Can I just take her? No, I couldn't. I should.

Maybe I won't keep her long. But she enraptures my thoughts. I doubt I will be able to sit still knowing someone so clear and pure is out there. It's honestly refreshing. She is like smoke. Oh, how rude of her to make it so easy. How rude of me to want her.

"Hey, Mr., I think this is yours." Her quiet voice rang through his ears, alarming his entire system. "I don't know, as I turned, it seemed you dropped this," the Damsel placed the paper from her hands to his, giving him a warm smile. "Thank you. I wonder why this fell out of my pocket. Right now?" "Maybe the timing is right. If wisdom is telling you something, then it's up to us to listen to that advice, no?"

"This may seem forward, but can I buy you some tea, maybe hot chocolate? On me." She checked her phone for the time, not sure if she should prolong this delightful conversation. "I would, but I am running a bit late. I work at the observatory up the block if you are interested in the stars." He smiled, honestly elated that she was enjoying his company and requesting more of it. "To be honest, I had no interest in the colors of space until now, but here," the man pulled out a pen and wrote a note on the previously fallen paper," smiled and tipped his hat, before walking away.

The woman smiled, waved, looking at the paper as she walked on.

Dear "Wisdom,"

If I could describe you. It would be colorless. But that isn't a bad thing, for I realized that you push out the most vivid sights and sounds from the words that emanate within. Hold on to that.

To color. And new beginnings.
Q.

P.S.
I would give you my number, but you are worth the effort. In seeing the stars.

—-

Diaz and Eli snuck down the fire escape and into the car. Eli handed him the letter, and as they zipped through the winding streets, Diaz looked at E, surprised. "I can't believe this. He is getting sloppy. This letter was almost spelling it out to you where she is."

"I know," replied Eli. That's what I'm afraid of Wis. It's too easy. As the duo pulled into the parking lot. They ran through the doors of "Glass Sky," the observatory. "I'll check around, you ask the lady at the front if they have seen your mom lately," Diaz urged before running up the stairs to get to the equatorial room.

Eli nodded and rang the bell at the desk to get the woman's attention. "Hey, Lady! Have you seen a woman in her 40s, short, African American, with features like mine?" The woman behind the desk thought for a while, testing Eli's patience as the seconds went on. "Yes, I have. She and a man went up to the telescope."

"Really! Did you see them leave together or the man at least?" He urged. "Sorry, no, when you get up there, can you tell them we are closing in ten?" Before she could get the rest of her statements out, Eli ran to catch up with Diaz. As he got to the top, he saw Diaz reaching under the telescope for something.

"Hey Diaz, what are you doing? The desk lady said my mom is supposed to be up here." Eli asked watching as the detective was straining, as if he was carrying a heavy object. "Come help!" Diaz screamed, causing Eli to jolt and run towards him. As he got closer, he caught the full view of his unconscious mother hanging from the bottom end of the telescope, where it was protruding out of the open window.

As Eli got closer, a figure grabbed him from behind. Before he could yell to Diaz for help, the man injected him with a tranquilizer to the neck, dropping his body on the floor. The masked man placed an envelope on his chest, before slipping out the door.

"Eli, wake up!"

He could feel a light shining on his face. It was warm, and he was annoyed that someone was disturbing his sleep. As he opened his eyes, he realized that he was back at home, on his couch. He recognized that the voice yelling at him to awake was his mother and without a second to spare he sprung up, not believing his senses just yet.

"Mom!" He leaped, hugging her in shock. "I saw you there unconscious, and then as I was coming to help, someone grabbed me and knocked me out." His mom chuckled in relief. "I know. Detective Diaz helped me out, and I am forever grateful for that. You must invite him over for dinner so I can say thank you." Eli nodded in obedience, "sure, where's Dad?" "He is outside on the phone with the police. You should go tell him you're awake; he was worried sick about you."

As Eli walked closer to the balcony, he heard another voice on the other end of his Dad's call. He knew he shouldn't eavesdrop but he couldn't help himself. "I understand sir. This won't happen again. I apologize."

It was Diaz's voice. Why was he apologizing? He saved everyone. Those women, his mom, him. If anything I should be the one who's sorry. Eli swung the sliding door back, foregoing his hiding spot, and jumped in front of his Dad. "Dad, why are you getting on Diaz? I am the one who is at fault. I endangered Mom and Hope, and myself."

"Elijah, this is getting out of hand." His father sighed. "Yeah, I know, but, Diaz did nothing wrong though. I would be dead or asleep somewhere if it weren't for him. He not only saved me, he dragged us both back here. Why are you punishing him?" Sighing, his Dad looked at his eager son, before returning to his phone, holding his hand up to silence his son. "Okay. I got it. See you soon, Diaz."

"What did I say about being impatient? I wasn't getting on Diaz. He called me to apologize for the danger you have been in. Now, I told him I appreciate the gesture, and for him to come by for dinner in a few days."

Eli looked at his Dad, surprised.

Maybe I am impatient?

Suspicion

Guess who's coming to dinner? Detective Diaz. And my parents are pulling out all the stops. "After the whole fiasco with my mom, my Dad, of all people invited him. It's the least we can do right," Eli said to Hope and Daniel on a three-way call. He was talking to them while surfing his computer reading up on the Mr. Q. forums.

"Yeah, I mean, he did save your mom. Also your Dad should seem super appreciative of him. Maybe if it goes well, then they will allow you to investigate that Q. guy," mentioned Daniel. Hope hummed in agreeance. Right, they don't know that this all occurred because I was helping Diaz in the first place. I think it is better to keep them out of the loop. I mean Hope just got back to school, and things are fairly normal now.

Whatever normal is.

Deep down I still have this blurry thought that I am forgetting something. Something important. My mind has been hazy since I woke up. Who was it that drugged me at the observatory? At first I thought it was Q., but how would I even know? Does he have an accomplice? Nah. he couldn't. He could, but this town has enough craziness going on with one killer. Bringing two in the mix and that would be borderline apocalyptic.

Knock. Knock. Knock. "Hey, I'll call you guys back, I think

they are here." Eli hurriedly shuts his laptop and runs towards the front door. "I'll get it!" When he opens the door he realizes that there are two. Not weird at all.

"Eli. How's it been? How is your mom?" asks Campbell as he carries in a bouquet. "Can you put this in a vase? It's for your mom." Taking the flowers, he asked, "Why do all cops knock the same? Is it some class you all take at the academy?" Campbell chuckled through the entrance motioning for Diaz to take the reigns of the conversation. "Yes, we all take a knocking class, E." Diaz answered, walking into the foyer, pie in hand.

"I almost forgot. Here, I went back to the observatory, and the lady at the kiosk gave it to me." It's a letter, and of course, it's addressed to me. "Thanks, I'll read it after dinner. I don't want to spoil my appetite with serial killer talk."

"Look at you getting wiser." Campbell added. "I try." As the three of them walk into the living room, Mr. Elliot walked in, knife in hand. "Ah, Detectives welcome!" "Careful, Dad, you almost stabbed Diaz."

"Sorry, I forgot this was in my hand," he said placing the knife on the table. "No problem, what's a stab to that right hook you gave me?" Mr. Elliot rubbed the back of his head, embarrassed. "Right, that was sloppy of me, sorry about that Detective."

Sloppy indeed Dad.

"Right, well enough of that awkwardness," Eli interjected. "Mom said dinner will be ready in a few minutes. I hope you guys like vegetarian." "Vegetarian? I always pegged you as a cow-eater, E," Campbell jests. "Nah, my parents detest the killing of animals. My Dad loves the environment. I think that's crazy talk considering he contributes to pollution everyday by driving taxis."

"Oh, your dad is a taxi driver," Diaz inquires. "What company?" Mr. Elliot placed some coasters on the table shaking his head at Eli's silliness. "I've worked for Hugh Motors since I was a young adult. So it's coming onto about twenty-five years this November." Diaz nodded in understanding, grabbing some napkins to help. "I know of that company. It used to be called Rainbow Roadways before it got bought out by that guy, right?" interjects Campbell.

"Yeah, we don't see the boss much, but I guess driving doesn't require that kind of interaction."

—-

BANG.

"Elijah Quincy Elliot! Why is there water all over the floor!?" Eli ran to the kitchen, apologizing, whilst grabbing the mop."Quincy?" Pondered Diaz. "Yeah, he is the fifth generation of Elijah's, so Quincy is his middle name." Chimed his dad. "Interesting. I always thought his middle name would have started with an E. Go figure," piped Campbell. Diaz found a seat at the dining room table, eyeing his surroundings. A piece of stationery stood out to him, and just as he was about to grab it, Mr. Elliot picked it up.

"Sorry about the mess, I got this from the guys at work. They are going to throw me an anniversary party since I am one of the oldest members around." "Can I see it? I love this kind of paper," asked the curious cop. "Sure, be my guest." Mr. Elliot passed him the letter and walked to grab some more glasses for the table.

As Diaz opened the letter, nothing stood out, it was a plain invitation, except for the kind of paper it was on. It had the same feel and weight as the ones Q. would send. "What if?" He pondered, contemplating if such a coincidence existed.

"What if what?" asked Eli now back in the Dining room, placing a tray of macaroni on the table. "Don't take this the wrong way, or be alarmed, but I think your Dad works with Mr. Q." Eli froze in shock, before a disappointed look donned his face. "That's rich, we invite you for dinner and you accuse my Dad of working with a serial killer. I thought we were getting closer, Detective. I mean, we even made you mac and cheese. My mom only cooks that on special occasions!" Eli ranted, upset with the accusation.

Diaz stood up in protest, trying to explain himself in a nervous-hushed tone. "No. Eli, I think Mr. Q. works at the taxi company with your Dad. Look, it's the same kind of paper. And didn't you tell me your Dad thought the letter Q. sent you when your Mom got taken was an invitation at first? That can't be a coincidence."

"Oh." Eli sighs in relief. "Makes sense, you scared me man. If what you are saying holds weight, then we should check it out then." "You mean I should?" Diaz curtly says. "Your parents just invited me for dinner, I am not ruining my chances by getting you kidnapped or killed. Your Dad can punch, you know."

"Right, right," Eli assured him, before going back into the kitchen. After a few minutes, everyone gathered back into the dining room. After grace, they sat down and began to indulge in their meals. "This is delightful, Mrs. Elliot, the best meal I've had in a while," Campbell uttered in between bites.

"I have leftovers for you two to take later," she stated, passing the basket of dinner rolls to Eli. "Thank you again, Detective, for saving me. I know Elijah can be a handful, but I feel better knowing he is learning some responsibility fro a capable person when he isn't at home."

"Of course, ma'am, Eli is like a little brother to me. I will make sure he doesn't get hurt." Diaz replied. "And how will you guarantee that?" Asked Mr. Elliot. "I don't trust you with my son, Detective. That Q. guy is always near him, and it seems you are always a step behind. Maybe two. Or three."

"Dad!" Eli chirped, embarrassed. "No, your Dad is right, E," interrupted Diaz. "Sir, your son will not be in any investigations anymore. I give you my word." His word. I didn't give mine. "No offense, but you seem to burn bridges around you. I can't watch my son be on the other side of that fire."

Diaz winced at his words, catching the attention of Campbell. "Hey, don't you think that is a little harsh, Mr. Elliot? Sure, Matthew has messed up, but we are very close to catching this killer."

"Is that so?" Mr. Elliot added, unimpressed. "Very so." "I can't say I believe you, Lieutenant Campbell. We are living in a rainbow of chaos. I don't think we can depend on such black and white statements. Especially when this has to do with my one and only child."

"Alright!" Eli interjected. "I am right here, you know. I won't be in any investigation with them. Happy?" "Very," added Eli's mom. "Mom," he whispered in shame. She ignored his pleas and turned towards the other three men at the table. "Now, who wants dessert? Detective Diaz bought a lovely pie."

—-

"Sorry about dinner. Please come again anytime." Eli sympathetically offered to the Detectives. "My parents are overprotective, and I am their only child. They don't understand the stress you guys have going on. They just want me safe. Sorry about that."Campbell laughed and Diaz shook his head in understanding. "Don't sweat it kid. It could have been much worse." Diaz spoke. "Right." added Campbell. "No dinner is complete without awkward conversations. And we have to be grateful. I haven't had a good meal like that in such a long time. Your mom is a fantastic cook. Plus they should be protective of you." Diaz put his coat on and turned back to the young man's apologetic face. "Eli, your Dad loves you a lot, and I know he is worried about you. No hard feelings there," he said.

"Oh, right, I almost forgot." Diaz pulled an envelope from his pocket and handed him a letter before stepping out the front door towards the car. Eli stood on the balcony as the entered their car and drove off. Eyeing as the vehicle grew smaller into the horizon, he took a deep breath, just taking in all of the moments that led up to today. How if he never went to the movies that one day, he would have never met Diaz and had him over for family dinner. After a few moments of fresh air, he walked back into the house, locking the front door behind him before towards his room. As he was placing the letter in his hand down on his desk, he realized there was already one there. Turning it over to read the cover, he noticed they both were addressed to him. Except one was from Q. and one from Diaz.

"If I didn't know any better, I would say these two were similar," whispered E. Two different sides of the same coin.

Regrets

I'm getting too popular, Wisdom.

I'm too much in the public eye and it's not helpful because I hate being the center of attention. But alas, it continues to follow me, along a path once cascaded with light but now a dark and murky tunnel that leads to who knows where, currently, stuck in the middle of right and wrong, good and evil. Diaz and Q.

I can't help but ponder if I should throw both of those letters away. Never read them, go back to school after a well deserved break, and forget that a serial killer is spiritually connected to me via a friend of my imagination. I don't mean to be so blunt in my thoughts but Wisdom, you are the only one I can talk to. My parents wouldn't get it. They might even check me into some psych ward. My friends just got out of danger so can't take that way, and Diaz is nice, but he is still a cop. I can't get to close to him.

Maybe I should just cut the story now, forego any foreshadowing, and live peaceably. I know, Wis, peace is earned. As Eli pulled the letters off his desk, he wondered if Diaz was also a little psycho because the envelope he gave was the same as Q.'s. "Do cops often adopt the tendencies of killers?" he whispered. I know, I'm stalling. Eli closed his eyes and opened a letter, not really caring who it was from of the two.

Dear Elijah the Earnest,

I should apologize to you. As I said, we are fairly similar. And taking your mother was a very difficult task — not one I would have gone through with if you hadn't goaded me on. But I am no monster — a man of my word. It wasn't difficult to take her physically but I think I may have emotionally wounded you and for that I am sorry. But don't you realize how unique you are? A perfect blend of clarity. Neither black nor white, red, blue, or any other color for that matter.

Perfectly transparent. Clear in character.

Yet you squander your talents by hanging with degenerates like Diaz and Campbell. Shame. I must warn you. If you still choose to chase impatiently after me. Then, at least have some decorum in your actions. You're bright, but your peers are dimming what little light you have left. Yes, dear Elijah, time is ticking, and you must decide.

Light or eternal darkness? Truth or the color of lies?

Unaccompanied,
  Mr. Q.

P.S.
  Stop lingering in the shadows before the darkness drags you down for good. Rise above yourself.

I have no words. Actually, I do. What the actual was that. Of course, only Q. could make an apology so creepy, also, why does this sound like a recruitment ad? I really don't know what to do with that first letter. Eli shook his head in disbelief and picked up the second, beginning to scan the scribbled language on the page.

To Eli,

Now, I know you are wondering why I am writing you a letter when the phone is a much easier option. I guess I should say that easy was never an option for me. Additionally, I may be learning a few things from Q. subconsciously. And what's worse is that I don't know if that is a good or bad thing, but so be it.

You are a good kid, better than I was at your age. But there is more to life than chasing the bad guys. I know, how can a cop tell you to run the other way? It's very hypocritical. But I see you as the son I would have had. He would have been four.

And as I see from a would be fatherly perspective, I can tell that you are teaching me the greatest lesson I could learn: that it is too late to regret when new issues arrive every day. So as long as we make the effort to do better, yesterday can linger in the past.

So in honor of that, during my next investigation don't come. I would like knowing that you are safe at home rather than getting an inch closer to some killer.

Diaz

And now I feel as if I was rejected from a job interview. Figures. But, I am in this whether they approve or not. From the moment my mother was taken it was on. No. Since the day I saw that woman die in that blue abyss. Even though it might be unwise to go in alone, at least I have you. Right Wisdom?

Eli tossed the letters in the trashcan near his desk before pulling a dark-colored hoodie on. He waited late into the night, with his ear pressed into the door, to hear if his parents went to sleep. Then he snuck out his window, down the fire escape into the cold air, in search for answers.

— -

Hugh Motors was dark. I mean, everything is dark when it's nighttime. Diaz told me to stay away, and I should have listened, as I feel the cool breeze attack the uncovered spots on my figure. I believe I acted too quickly this time. So, you scream if anything goes wrong. I'm kidding. I'll scream. My legs are beginning to ache, and if I am being honest, I have been walking for miles now and I still don't know where I am going. What is a taxi company supposed to look like? I thought it would be a gated place with a bunch of cars, but now I wonder if I am in the right place.

Eli turned into a semi-secluded part of the city. As he walked, his feet shuffled swiftly against the rough gravel. Every few steps he kicked cans in his way due to boredom. Then he saw his destination and turned into a decrepit parkway. "This is where my Dad works?" He muttered, disappointed. How depressing; it's so dark and empty, leading me to believe that his long hours on the road are to avoid coming back to a workplace like this. Taxis lined up awaiting their drivers.

I am not sure what I will find here, but I think this is my only chance to help, because if I know Diaz, he would most likely be here any day with the police to turn over every stone and spare tire. With that, I think the first step to finding clues is breaking in. Don't worry Wis, I didn't learn these skills by vandalizing places and such. Twenty bucks, the internet, and a lock-picking kit later, I am inside.

Now, where would a killer keep clues of his crimes at his workplace? Would they keep it here? An idiot would, but I doubt Q. would. Maybe it's his accomplice? Does he have one? Am I the accomplice of a killer now? If I don't answer those letters, does that mean they think I said yes to the both of them?

Probably so. Eh, that's alright, I doubt my decision would change the course of this entire thing. And with that, quick question, Wis. Why is Q. so obsessed with the concept of color, or should I say the lack of it? The man is too strange to comprehend. Which proves two things. One, I am the newfound interest of a killer. Great. And two, I am way in over my head with this. I need help.

Eli pulled out his phone and messaged a number that could shine some light on this whole thing. About thirty minutes later, a car pulled up, and a man stepped out after cutting his headlights off. "Hey! Anyone here?" The man questioned into the darkness. "Psst. Over here." Eli piped. "Man, for a cop, you sure are loud."

"Eli, this is beyond stupid man, but I am glad you called, instead of doing this by yourself," Campbell responded, using his flashlight, shining it in his overall direction. "C'mon, Campbell. Be serious, and put that light away." Campbell nodded and turned off the flashlight. "Look, I got two letters and both seemed like horrible options, so I figured you would be a better option to talk to. Please don't make me regret it." Campbell laughed and walked closed to the building door ignoring the jumpy teen.

Elijah gestured into the unlocked entrance and closed the

door behind them both. "I take it the door was unlocked before you got here?" "Huh? Yeah, it was magically unlocked the night I decided to do a solo, I mean duo, investigation. Very lucky." I don't think he bought it. But like I said Wis, very lucky.

"Anyway, I have a question for you. How long has it been since the last victim showed up dead?" Eli asked sitting on a chair near some desk "I would say roughly two and a half weeks, considering the last victim who died was because of the police. But if we are talking Q. induced, then roughly a month ago. Why?"

"I don't want to seem grim," he said, "but isn't it on par for another one to show up? It has been a while, do you think he is blood-hungry?"

—-

Eli rummaged through files on a desk before stumbling on a letter. At first, it seemed like the invitation his Dad had received from his colleagues, but something about this stood out to him. Mainly, the fact that his name and Diaz's name were on it. Not as a package but rather separate entities.

To whom finds me first. Elijah or Diaz.

Either there was a camera on me, or Q. was a very paranoid person. As Eli walked towards Campbell to show him the inscribed paper, a very distinct smell wafted through the air, going unnoticed by the both of them. Instead Eli focused on the letter, and got up to show his investigating partner. "Campbell, look. This was waiting for me and Diaz, regardless of who was going to find it first."

"Well, come on my friend. Open it! I think that was all that was intended to be here; I can't make sense of anything else here, so read it and let's head out." Eli agreed just as Campbell pulled up two chairs and scooted the lamp on the table closer to them in order to get a good look.

To whom finds me first. Elijah or Diaz.

I have been watching, watching the watchers. I know, how original. But who I am doesn't concern you. What I am going to do does. Just know, I don't like sharing the sun. I don't like offering up my toys.

I was given a very specific task. Something that will tie me in with the flames and burn all you have worked up to. That being nothing, as the blind lead the blind in this story.

A partner should never be overlooked. And despite Wisdom never answering my call. I demand to be looked at. I am growing tired of Q. getting all the shine, when I do most of the grunt work. So now I will take and offer him my gifts. A sidekick's contribution.

Diaz and Eli vs. Q. and I.

Again, who I am is irrelevant. Just remember I can touch the stars without being unscathed. I can't say the same for you.

"That's it? No name, not even the same writing style. What gives?" Eli pushed back his chair in annoyance, considering his time wasted because there were no other clues found. He looked at Campbell who was deep in thought, not caring anymore and walking back to the entrance.

"So Q. has a partner, and we have no insight into who. Maybe a colleague?" Campbell paced the floor in thought before stopping abruptly. "What's that smell?" "Smell? Campbell, if you need fresh air, just say so." Elijah grabbed the handle of the door, not minding the obvious warning in the air. "Wait! I don't think you should do that, El-" Campbell reaches forward too late as an explosion hits the entrance of the cab company, blowing himself and Eli to the ground.

Aflame

Wis?

Wisdom, help me.

Elijah awoke hazy, under a cloud of smoke with flames surrounding the building. As he tried to get up his neck restricted much movement, headache taking priority over the situation he was in. 'Campbell.' He thought, ignoring the pain he was in. Turning behind him to see what became of the cop, he was almost struck by falling rubble due to the building burning above.

"Campbell!" He coughed amidst the thickening smoke, realizing that the smell before was gas, and that he nearly died opening a door. How dumb. But it was indication that they were on the right track and that he was getting too close to this. Wisdom, do you see Campbell? I need to know if he is safe. Diaz will kill me. Everyone will kill me, and no matter what I do it is putting me in a dangerous situation. If that isn't a curse, then I don't truly know the definition of the word.

'Focus,' he said, snapping himself out of his thoughts. "Campbell, come on man! Where are you. Are you okay?" In the far corner of the rubble he noticed his friend, and limped across the room, tripping over much debris, and lifting the obstacles in front of him that he could to get closer to the kind detective.

Hearing the sirens in the distance made him want to move even faster. He didn't do anything worth trouble, but he knew the police would come and blow the lid on this entire thing. Maybe he could find Campbell's body before that happens. He was getting too close to this case, and if Campbell was dead. If. Then there would be no doubt that the authorities would get fed up with the whole thing, and take the easy route of blaming everything on him. A young African American, centered amid five or so different killings/kidnappings, was like handing himself over as a statistic.

"Campbell. Man, Campbell, Are you okay?" He yelled weakly a few more times before approaching a body on the floor, knocked out. As he paced faster, holding his sleeve up to his face to block out further smoke, a figure jumped out behind him and grabbed him swiftly.

Elijah began kicking as if he were wading through large currents, drifting farther and farther apart from the helpless body upon the ground. "No, no, you don't understand! Help him! He could die, and it's not his fault. You have to help him! Help H-" Wait. Eli froze. He looked closer at the person on the floor. His realization alarmed him. That wasn't Campbell. That's not him. It was, a woman?

How is that even possible? There was no one else but them there, he made sure of it before he looked for clues. With this deduction he began wondering who was carrying him, and who is lying on the floor, life slipping away? Where was Campbell? Who is that woman on the ground?

"I am going to die. Aren't I?" He asked not sure if he was confirming it within himself or asking this kidnapper. Just that the question was full of fear. "Sorry, my friend, not quite. We have some unfinished business to discuss." The masked person, with a voice disguise on, spoke with such chilling vibrato. Eli couldn't respond after that, accepting his fate, whatever that may be.

—-

Diaz was sound asleep for the first time in years. Drifting into his dream, a familiar image popped into his head. It was what he yearned for after a long day and it always the same;

"Hi. I am Officer Diaz. I believe this is yours, Ms.?" He handed the purse to the flushed woman, trying to catch her breath. "Take your time, there are no more bad guys. Um Maybe I could get you something? Some water?" He politely offered. "No. No," she smiled through her breaths. "Thank you, Officer, I thought my stuff was gone forever." She replied grabbing the bag from his hands, and rummaging through it for her inhaler. "How can I repay you for this? Do you want to get a coffee, maybe a doughnut?"

He chuckled. "Doughnuts, funny. I will take you up on that coffee though. A bit chilly out. Are you sure you are okay?" "Yes," she declared, taking a puff of the medication in order to calm her attack. "I know it was foolish to run after that guy in my condition but I just got it refilled this morning. The timing couldn't be worse."

"Oh yeah that is a hassle, glad I was in the area." He looked around before continuing. "I don't mean to state the obvious but we are in the middle of the street. Let's get you that coffee, huh?" "Right Right! Sorry. My name is Gia. Gia Campbell." She stretched her hand out to shake his. He smiled at her cute expression and grabbed her hand in response, moving to the nearest sidewalk. "The name's Diaz, Matthew Diaz."

His dreams always began that way, sweet, warm, and everything nice, before turning into his biggest nightmare. His worst truth.

—-

She's gone isn't she? No, I can't think that way. I just had to work today, and I just so happened to not have my phone around when she called. Everything should be fine right? Maybe, it's just a false alarm. Man, why didn't I have my phone on me? What is wrong with me? Diaz's thought continued to spiral as he walked into the station, rushing with his things so he could grab a taxi to the Hospital.

"Hey, it will be okay," spoke Campbell hopping in the taxi on the opposite side. "You think? I hope she's okay. Rain too." Diaz put his head in his hands. "I am a terrible person." "No. Look, she should be fine, and I spoke earlier. Gia said the baby and she were going to be fine and she was waiting for you," Campbell added.

"Really," he sighed, calming the panic in his voice. "How long ago was this?" "About a few hours ago. The doctors took her phone, but she should be fine." Right, he thought to himself. She should be okay. Maybe this was first-time parent jitters, but he had a deep feeling that things were not so good. He didn't want to think to hard on that possibility, because if things were going south, then he really wouldn't know what to do.

Trying to ease his mind he pulled his phone out and dialed her number again.

—-

Ring.
Ring.
"Hello?"
He awoke in a cold sweat, checking the clock not fully sure he was hearing things correctly. "Detective, we need your help." The person on the other line stated, forcing him to jump up.

As he grabbed his things he couldn't help but panic slightly. Campbell was all he had left, and Eli. Well, Eli felt like his second chance. A second chance at normalcy, at being a Dad. And knowing they both could be gone was a thought he tried not to entertain too long on, in fear of throwing up.

"I'm on my way, give me the location." He spoke, before shutting his door. Picture frame falling to the ground, cracking further more.

—-

If I find out you are in on this I will never forgive you. I know you hear me, Wis. I need help. As Eli tugged at his restraints he recognized that he was in the same room that Hope described when she got kidnapped. Childlike yet sterile. The only difference was that now it was him in this predicament. In the back of his mind, he felt slightly relieved that only he was in danger, not pulling anyone else into this sick game. But where was Campbell? 'I hope he is okay,' he thought. He imagined his parent's faces as their only child was in danger, realizing that in a few years, they would be too old for drama like this. Hoping he would get to see them soon, safely.

"Hello? Anyone here." He shouted into the pristine atmosphere, shocked the operations of a killer were quite clean. "Q. I know this isn't your plan. I mean you just sent me a letter about being on your side. We can try to discuss things further." He bluffed not sure if what he was saying was going to dig him into a deeper hole. Hopefully not six feet under.

"For someone who just woke up you talk a lot." The masked man responded, rubbing his face in annoyance. "Keep quiet, the fun will begin in just a moment." Eli tugged at his restraints. "Look man, I didn't see your face. I don't know who you are but you can't just let me go, and then we can go about our own business. Deal?" E pleaded.

Another masked figure walked in quickly, throwing down a weighty hammer. "What did I say? I wanted Diaz! Not him but the Detective." He yelled across the room, echoes of anger bouncing off the walls. "Well I assumed if we have him, then we have Diaz. They are a package deal, and really what's the problem anyway? If he does anything dumb we can kill him. Your first male victim. Sounds fun?"

"No, I hate the recklessness. Are you really in this?" The leader questioned. "Because you are quite replaceable. If your hatred is not directed clearly, then, we can cut our losses now, and I will do this on my own."

"No! I will not go astray anymore. Sorry Q." Eli stared in bewilderment of their dynamic. So of course the boss is Q., but who is this guy? Wis, did you know he had a sidekick? "I don't understand this, if you're Q., then who is this wannabe?" Eli inquired, shifting in his seat, not even sure if he truly wanted to know the answer. Q. shrugged mockingly before walking out. Turning his attention to the other masked figure, he replied, "tell him if you want, it doesn't change my plans anyway."

The first masked man nodded, closed the door behind Mr. Q., and pulled his mask up. Eli would have never guessed. "It can't be! But I thought you were," Eli gasped. "Dead. No. No my friend. This game is just beginning, poor Eli. We do have to wait a little, we are missing a fellow person. Diaz, I mean," muttered the man. Looking at the moody assistant's face it was clearly a man, a man none other than Campbell.

Are you seeing this, Wisdom?

Reasons

I don't get it.

"What could your motive possibly be to betray your brother-in-law?" Eli shouted at the man formerly unmasked, not truly accepting the changed narrative of this story. Campbell shuffled around the room. Silent for a while, which caused Elijah's anxiety to skyrocket. Q. left him with this man who was once a friend, and somehow that felt far worse than any wickedness he felt from the initial villain.

"Eli, poor Eli. I always had this mentality. Diaz was just too dumb to realize that his actions don't only impact the dead. The living have to be the ones to pick up the pieces. Honestly, how unfair of him to live peaceably while the innocent pay for his crimes over and over again." Campbell found a seat on a chair. Amusingly, tapping his legs, smiling at Elijah's continuing confusion.

"Okay, to be very honest, that is the dumbest thing I have heard in a while. I mean, you paired up with a killer for what? Revenge? How outdated." Eli sighed, hoping his grasp at conversation would stall Campbell until help came. "You don't understand, I am the one who recruited Q. He may think we are playing his game, but I have been the one pulling the strings." So he's delusional and disloyal. Got it.

"So what you are saying is that you never cared for Diaz at all?" Campbell shook his head in agreement. "Isn't that a long time to hide the way you feel about someone, especially an enemy?" Eli was getting unsatisfied with Campbell's answers. He felt hurt on Diaz's behalf, no one should have to experience this kind of heartbreak, and the wildest thing of it all was that Diaz had no clue. No clue at all that his best friend hated his guts.

"I don't know. That's a bad look, Campbell. Even for a psycho like Q., he wouldn't stoop that low. I mean, there is a lot I am missing story-wise, so please convince me that what you are saying is true. Give me your side of things." Eli urged, sitting up in his chair for a better look at the man before him. He was determined to get some concrete answers out of the man, thinking it would help him if he survived until the authorities arrived. Wis, am I destined to be intertwined with the psychotics of the world? I think after all of this I need to go on a very long vacation. Maybe the mountains where there is lots of snow.

"Hey! Focus! I know you are talking to that Wisdom entity or whatever, and I find it rude that you can't listen when you asked me a question." Like I said, he is crazy. "Last warning! Q. said I can't kill you, but I don't think he would mind much if I bent the rules a little." Elijah didn't like the sound of that. Campbell annoyed now, pulled his chair closer, knife in hand, only millimeters away from Eli's neck. "Alright, Alright! I'm listening." E pleaded, wondering if Campbell was also involved in Hope's kidnapping, or the killing of all those women.

"Nice try, but I won't give you all the details now," laughed the Lieutenant. We can't spoil our appetites when the Guest of Honor is still missing. Don't worry, knowing him, he will find us soon." Elijah gulped at that response, feeling the stainless steel occasionally prick at his jugular. He was too focused on not breathing too hard to protest against Campbell, fear lacing the air with the knife's sharpness.

"I don't have anyone left." Campbell continued. "And I gave Diaz a very precious gift, that he squandered for his ambitions. So I implored Q. after the murder in the forest. Yes way back then, and watched as the chaos ensued." Campbell let up on the knife and turned, hearing the door open behind him, placing his mask back on in a hurry.

"Ah, Elijah! I see you are alert now. How nice of you to be here. I would have liked it to be of your own volition and under better circumstances, but beggars can't be choosers." Q. sauntered in again, happier than before while Eli didn't lift his head to look at Q., he raised no further emotion to his quips. Not wanting to satisfy this erratic killer. "I know you have a lot of questions, and thankfully, I am feeling generous. So I will allow you to ask only one. Choose very wisely."

I don't know about this Wisdom, what should I ask him?

—-

Diaz was beside himself. All he ever loved was taken from him time and time again. What even was his purpose, if everything he did ended in flames and destruction? As he rummaged through the remains of the cab company, there wasn't much to go through. Most of it was rubble and scattered debris. The bomb wasn't a large one, so the integrity was still there, just under a layer of ash. He was told that when the first responders arrived they found a woman and declared her dead before the fire occurred. Again, confirming in his mind that Q. was killing victims and then dropping them off in other locations. What a sick tendency.

As he continued to dig, something stood out amidst the dying flames. Something dark and shiny. Picking it up, he noticed it was cool to the touch, though slightly melted along the sides. 'Eli had to be here,' he deduced, examining what he thought was a lock-picking tool further. Putting it in an evidence bag, he pushed more stuff out of the way, convinced he was on the right track. A track that hopefully led to his family being safe.

This went on for hours. Officers periodically checked in on Diaz, pleading that he should take a break. But the more they begged him to take it easy, the more he felt as if the lead was slipping farther from him. Eli and Campbell with it. Then he saw it. A partially burnt letter, donned in the same fashion as all the others Q. had sent before. He examined it, his face full of confusion because the writing was so foreign. Q. was a madman, but he kept a pattern just for the fun of it. This language felt like a virus, unwelcome and invasive in this game Diaz was dragged unwillingly into.

"What do you have there, Diaz?" Urged the Captain, frustrated with the lack of progress in this case. "A letter, but it isn't from Q." Diaz replied. "Well, then it's useless. Let another wave of officers search for clues," commanded the Captain.

"Sorry, Cap. I meant to say that it is relevant. It seems to be from another person in this situation. Like a fourth player emerging from the shadows." "Well, what can you make of it?" the Captain questioned. 'I'm not sure,' thought Matthew. He began scanning the document, looking for anything that stood out.

Who I am is irrelevant. Just remember I can touch the stars without being scathed. I can't say the same for you.

Stars? Was that a clue to the observatory? Diaz read the words carefully but felt like he was missing a very important clue.

I don't like sharing the sun. I don't like offering up my toys.

Something that will tie me in with the flames and burn all you have worked up to. That being nothing, as the blind lead the blind in this story.

A partner should never be overlooked.

Diaz and Eli vs. Q. and I.

Diaz shut the letter in his hands. "Hey Captain, I'm done here for now. I need to get back to the station. I think I have a lead." Diaz grabbed his things and hopped in his patrol car, not minding the slurry questions the Captain spat at him in the blur of it all.

Back at the station, he surrounded himself with clues about the previous murders. The one that always stood out to him was the Green murder—the one with the eerie question mark in the forest. He grabbed a photo from a pile of papers and walked up to a fellow officer's desk within the Archives, showing them the picture. "Have you seen this image before?" He urged, realizing he was out of options, but something kept tugging at him slightly, leading him on the correct path.

"Hmm. I don't know what is going on there, but it looks like it's near that place that burned down," the officer responded. "What building? I'm not a native here, care to teach a quick history lesson?" Diaz pleaded. "That's the orphanage that burned to the ground. A fire happened a while ago. No survivors though. It is a very tragic piece of history."

Campbell came to his mind. Then Gia. He grabbed a pen and flipped the photo around, not caring that he was defiling official evidence. "Can you give me the address?" The officer shrugged and wrote the directions to the Happy Colors Behavioral and Mental Health Center for Children, passing the photo back to Diaz before returning to their previous work.

"Thanks!" shouted Diaz, running to his car, hoping he wasn't too late.

—-

Q. and Campbell were getting tired of waiting for a response and prepared to exit the room. "Wait. I have one!" Eli shrieked. "What does family mean to you?" "Wow, Elijah, I knew you were a good choice, you know how to ask the most important things. I am impressed. I mean I certainly expected it but nonetheless I am impressed." Q. piped, pleasantly surprised. "Come on, I asked my question, enough with the compliments. You said you would answer. I thought you were a man of your word?" Eli sighed, fed up with the whole ordeal.

Whack.

Campbell smacked Eli, grabbing him by the shoulder so he could punch him, but Q. stepped in, placed his hand on Campbell's shoulder and pulled him away. "Campbell, my friend. You're getting very agitated, and it is scaring our guest. Right, Elijah?" Turned Q., watching as the young man sat quietly.

"I think he got the message. Anyway, he said turning his attention back to Eli. "To answer your question, family is everything. Life, death, and all substances in between." How poetic Eli thought sarcastically. Q. ignored the rude face donning him and continued with his taunting. "Did you know I have a son around your age?" "Does he know that you are a killer?" Eli muttered. "No, he doesn't. I don't mix business and pleasure. And don't think I forgot that you asked me two questions just now. I must punish you for that. Hmm, what should that be?" Q. paced slowly, tapping his temple in question.

Ignoring Q. and his never-ending punishments. He returned his head toward Campbell. "Hey. I never got an answer. What does family mean to you?" Campbell looked at Eli longingly, as if he was truly contemplating his response. Before he could indulge the answer, the door swung open, a figure bolted through the entrance, gun in hand. "Diaz!" yelled Eli, relieved with his friend's arrival. Amidst all of this commotion, Elijah looked around and realized that Q. was oddly not there anymore.

Campbell within all of that, ran, grabbing his knife in the process, and placed it in the same position as before on Eli's neck, stooping lower to whisper into his ear.

"If you must know, family means nothing to me. Nothing at all."

Exposed

"Diaz, my friend, you are late. Thank you for joining us, even if you don't seem to value time like we do. Eli here, was very close to being at my beck and call. Pity. Maybe next time." Q.'s voice rang from the intercom, vibrations echoing off the walls. "Eli, just sit still," Diaz spoke towards the young man, pointing his gun at the masked figure. All he could focus on was the knife inching near his throat.

"I don't know who you are but you don't have to do this. He is a good kid, and he doesn't deserve to be frightened like this. We can be civil, and talk like men." The masked villain didn't budge, instead pointing the knife closer until the sharpness pierced the skin, with Eli gritting his teeth in pain. "Alright! Alright! Look I'll even put my weapon down." Diaz shouted, as he slid his gun across the ground. It stopped at Eli's feet but he dared not to acknowledge it just as the man pulled the blade back. "That's sweet, but there is really no need. I have him and you right where I want you. Weapon or no weapon. Now I advise you to sit Detective, for what you will find will haunt you like it often haunts me."

Eli knew he should tell Diaz that it was Campbell under the mask, but he also knew that a knife at his neck was dangerous. It was an excruciating way to die indeed, and that little prick from earlier was all the warning he needed to not push his luck. So he decided to keep quiet and watch as the events in front of him unfolded.

Wis, what should I do? It feels like whatever decision I make calls for me to speak up or stay quiet. As if I have all the information in the world in my hands but with giving it away my fingers suffer. I'm honestly scared this won't end well, and I'm still useless because of this blade against my neck.

"Okay, I'll sit." Diaz grabbed a chair, dragging it closer, before taking a seat. He eyed the exits and the various intercoms around him while scooting the chair in front of Elijah. He wondered how much time he had to stall before the rest of his backup would come. Cautious not to think to hard of what could have happened to Campbell.

Q. having a sidekick was definitely a shock, it surprised him that this infamous killer needed additional help. Almost as if the smoke was starting to clear and he was getting a full look, finally, at the details of this case. Snapping back into focus, he turned his attention and stared straight at Eli's eyes not giving the Masked Man any satisfaction. He examined his terrified eyes, the various bruises on his body, and then the cut around his neck. Lastly, he looked at the knife in the Man's hand, noticing something. To the naked eye it was nothing but to Diaz it meant everything. Within the shaped steel he could see an engraved G and D on the blade. His heart sank. 'It couldn't be,' he thought. There was only one of its kind in the entire world.

—-

"You'll need it when I am not around okay? For your protection, in case he doesn't act right." Campbell said giving Gia her wedding gift. "A gift, thank you so much!" Gia tore the wrapping paper and opened it carefully. Inside laid a knife with gold specs within the blade, subtle writing as well, and engraving with her new initials.

"I don't think I would need it but regardless I love it. Thank you, Campbell." He smiled in response to her gratitude and lowered his head, eyes catching their matching rings. "Nice blade John, but come on. I would never hurt her, her protection is top priority. And who's to say I don't need it? She might hurt me." Diaz joked, earning a playful push from his new wife. "Thank you for allowing me to be a part of the family Campbell, It means the world to me." Diaz smiled holding her hands tightly. Campbell unimpressed, continued to stare at the couple's hands, recalling the day he first met her.

—-

Campbell still masked, noticed Diaz's frantic stares. "Pretty right? I got it from a very dear person of mine. Sadly, they aren't around anymore. And the world is starting to forget them, I hope you remember them. I wonder, do you remember Gia, Matthew?"

—-

Gia was the first to call him that. Campbell. He saw her at the orphanage when they were little kids. She was the new victim in the building, and just as children do, they began teasing her. He couldn't allow her to be mistreated, she was so small and looked very scared.

"I think I should help her." He urged. "C'mon Q. she looks scared." Unamused by the topic his friend shrugged. "If you help her then she will always ask you for stuff. Sharing sucks." Q. muttered turning back to his toys uninterested in the struggles of his peers. "But you share with me." He argued, before continuing, "that's okay if you ignore me now. I always wanted a little sister to take care of." Little Q. raised an eyebrow, but paid no mind to his friend's heroic tendencies. Young Campbell annoyed, got up and ran in her direction, shooing the other children away.

"Hi, I am John. John Campbell. My mom said it was like Bond, the super spy, but special, just for me. That was before she died though." He held his hand out nicely to help her up. "Hi, I am Gia. I don't think I have a last name. I guess my parents forgot." She laughed, standing up and dusting off her dress. "Well then Gia you can be a Campbell." He continued to hold her hand, walking her over to his table where Q. played. "This is my friend Q. He is pretty cool, even if he is a bit weird."

"His name is Q.? Like the letter?" She questioned. "That's my middle name. I was named after my father. But he isn't around anymore. My mom too." Q. never looked in their direction still playing with his undivided attention on his toys.

"She would have liked you, Gia. I can feel you. Your color is so clean. Like snow." Gia smiled, sitting down. "Snow is cool," she giggled. "What is your color Q.?" Campbell's smile fell. He leaned towards her before muttering a whisper. "He doesn't have one. At least that's what he told me." She clutched her dress in embarrassment, "Oh. Well that's okay, what about Campbell? What's his color?"

"His color is black. Very scary." Q. bluntly spoke, finally turning his face, staring at her, directly in the eyes. "It is very dark inside. I almost feel bad for him." Gia shivered, causing Campbell to jump in anger. "Hey man, don't scare her! He is just kidding, okay?" "Yeah, I am just kidding. It's not scary at all. Not to me." Q. felt a little bad about scaring her and passed the new girl a toy. "Here."

"Thank you," she smiled widely, holding on to the plush

elephant. "I love elephants. Gray is my favorite color." "I think so too, gray is cool." Chimed Campbell grabbing more toys from the table. "Well it's not. I think it is ugly. So gray." Q. whined, unhappy.

Very gray indeed.

—-

"How do you know about Gia? Just who are you?" Diaz was confused. Violated in a way. How could this killer have so much knowledge of him? How did he even get that knife? Gia's knife. It was locked up in a box within his closet. Along with everything else of his wife's, because he couldn't bear to throw anything of hers away.

That means that this person got into his house, without sounding or tripping the alarms and cameras. Who? Then it dawned on him. There was only one person who could have access to his home. One person that was currently missing. Or was he? Could he really be the masked figure in front of him? No. That's impossible. Maybe.

Eli could see the gears turning in Diaz's mind. He wanted to yell, tell him that what he thought was going on was true. Taking a quick chance, he cleared his throat. "Hey. Since I am not the real reason for all of this, just a decoy to get the detective here. Can I get a call? You can watch me. I just need to tell my parents that I am okay."

"You think I would fall for that. If you keep pushing your luck and you'll end up like that woman at the cab company." Campbell shouted. "Okay well, can you at least call her? It's not like you haven't met her. Remember the dinner? You loved her mac and cheese, right?" Eli said, hoping Diaz would catch on with such little information.

Diaz knew, and had a face of sadness. He caught onto what Eli suggested and felt it in his heart that this couldn't end well. What even was Campbell's motive for all this? How could he get out of this situation before Eli got hurt? Where was Q.? He had so many questions. "I don't understand. You invite me in and hold a knife to Eli's neck? You didn't even tie me up. Honestly, aren't you a bit worried that I would do something stupid, like call backup for some help? I mean, I still have my walkie on me."

Campbell thought for a while before taking the blade off Elijah's neck. Whew. I thought I was a goner Wis. He sauntered to the table and grabbed a bunch of rope, looking forward at Diaz the entire time, eyes full of hatred. Walking towards the Detective he knelt and began tying him up. As he continued to knot the rope around his wrists, Eli was steadily untying his restraints, trying his hardest not to make any noise.

Noticing that Campbell was distracted, he mouthed to Diaz his plan. Diaz nodded and coughed before speaking. "So what is your plan? I mean you tie us up. Possibly kill me after a long monologue, then kill Eli?" "Yes, precisely. Way to catch on."

"That's foolish. Doesn't Q. want Eli alive? Why would you jeopardize your dealings with Q. by taking out Eli?" He asked confused. "Because Q. is blinded by curiosity. I have shared before, and it ended in a loved one dying. I would be stupid to not kill him and end up dying instead." Campbell added still focused with the rope. Don't I get a say? Why is the topic shifting to my demise? Eli rolled his eyes, slowly reaching into his pocket, realizing that there was still a few pieces of his lockpicking kit there. He held on to the silver, waiting until Diaz signaled him to go.

"Is that because of Gia? She would not want you to go down

this path." Diaz added. This caused Campbell hesitate a little, then he continued tying. "She is no longer here to judge me. I am too far gone to consider my actions now. You think you are so smart. Don't try to get under my skin, because between the two of us, I think you have more skeletons in your closet. Like this knife."

Diaz was ready to signal Eli, just as Q.'s voice echoed into the intercom. "Diaz and Elijah, you two are sneaky. But not as sneaky as our masked fellow. Why keep us in suspicion? I think everyone already knows anyway. Don't we get to see what's under that mask?" Campbell sighed and stood up, unmasking himself. As he was working on that, Diaz yelled 'Go' to Elijah, who jumped up and kicked Diaz's chair back, breaking it, before running and upturning a table and crouching behind it.

Diaz loosened himself from the ropes and leaped on Campbell, tackling him in the process. They both fought tooth and nail, delivering blows to the body and face, reaching for the gun on the ground. While they were distracted Eli stayed crouched looking around. He spotted the exit and ran towards the door, inches away from freedom, before a loud ring filled the air.

Bang.

As Eli turned around he saw a pool of blood and Diaz holding his rib in pain. He could just run away. Get the police and crack this whole case wide open. But then Diaz would die, and that was something he was not willing to accept. He ran back into the commotion, not giving an mind to thinking a plan through.

As Campbell was preoccupied he jumped and stabbed his shoulder with the lock tool, before he got backhanded and knocked to the ground. He stumbled trying hard to get up, holding onto the agonizing pain emanating from the left side of his dome. Campbell then took the pistol and whipped him on the opposite side of his face, knocking him clean out.

Family

"I should just rid myself of all this and kill the both of you." Campbell pulled the mini tool out of his shoulder, tossing it in the direction of the wounded Diaz. He stared at him, trying his hardest not to lose consciousness, as he lost more blood with each second that passed . He turned his head slightly watching as Campbell stepped over him and dragged Eli's body closer, before grabbing his gun and pointing it at the unconscious college student. He winced trying to reach forward to stop him, slumping back, because the pain was too much to bear.

"You don't have to do this. I mean Gia wouldn't want this. John, she adored you. I saw you as the big brother I never had. Why are you doing this?" He winced. "Don't talk to me about Gia. Don't patronize me! I considered being helpful but you scorched her. All of your unluckiness rubbed off on her, and now she is dead. Your love had to die. Everything dies in the hands of Matthew Diaz!"

He boiled with anger, emotion spilling over. Diaz's face made him angry and he kicked the side of Eli's body in retaliation, eliciting a reaction from the shot detective. He sat down on a chair, gun pointed at Diaz now, before continuing. "She was the best of all of us, and she had to die. And now you have Elijah here," he scoffed, "and you want to play family with him, while your wife and real son haven't even been in the ground for longer than five years. This is on you Diaz."

"So that's it? You just kill more until you get your way. Then when Q. gets mad, you turn on him and just evade the police forever. Grow up, John." Diaz yelled, watching Eli before he shifted his attention back to Campbell, continuing his speech. "Gia died. I wasn't there but I was a good husband. And I will have to live with that for the rest of my life. But what can I say, other than the fact that I was late." His eyes were filling with tears remembering the day he lost her. Blinking back his sadness, he looked Campbell coldly in the eyes. "But you. You're just jealous because you couldn't have her. I think I always knew how you felt. But I just ignored that for her sake. She chose me and you would forever be only her brother. Her big brother John Campbell."

Q. silently watched through his video. Amused and surprised at the turn of events. He knew Campbell was unstable but that was the fun of his character. Ever since he was young he knew Campbell had a certain darkness to him. That's what made it so easy to be his friend, but when Gia came along he softened. "I guess that is the cost of loving someone. They become your weakness." He thought.

Q. turned his attention to Elijah, not sure if he should intervene. He originally wanted to toy with the child but Elijah dying would be a rather tragic tale. So much potential would be lost, and Campbell was too untrustworthy for him to believe he wouldn't lay a hand on the young man. Q. smiled, a bit tickled at everything happening. He rose up from his chair and shut the door behind him, thoughts solidified in a plan for the final act.

—-

"I don't understand G, you got your bag stolen and some random cop helped you. Why does that have to end with you going on a date with him?" Campbell took her coat placing it on the rack, leading her into the kitchen to take a seat. "I wouldn't call it that Campbell. It's gratitude." She said shuffling her bag and things into the nearby stool. "I mean he missed breakfast because of me, and then when I offered to get him something to eat at a nearby cafe, he got called into the station. So now I am having lunch with him tomorrow, as a thank you. It's not a date."

Gia began cutting vegetables at the counter, turning to the sink to rinse her hands. "Okay," he replied skeptically. "What's his name? Maybe I know him?" Campbell didn't really care but hid his jealousy by sitting down and stealing a carrot off the cutting board. "His name is Diaz." Gia mentioned before tapping his hand, so that she could scrape the remaining vegetables into a pan to saute and season them.

"Matthew Diaz? Not him. He is such a loner Gia. The guy is a weirdo honestly." He was lying through his teeth, well not at the loner part. That guy was a bit strange in the way he acted. "Well, aren't we all in some ways? I was a loner before I met you, and Q. is still a loner, wherever or whoever he is now." Gia shook her head thinking about her childhood, while stirring a pot full of sauce.

"Forget Q." John retorted. "Don't change the subject on me. I told you that I don't want you with a cop. They drag work home with them. There's no work-life balance whatsoever." He added before dumping a box of pasta into a roaring boil. "Hey! That's not fair. I think you forget that you are a cop, and you seem to do a good job of separating those two. Plus, what is to say that a guy in another career doesn't lack the ability to separate work and life? That seems like a problem everyone has."

She stopped her stirring and grabbed some plates from a nearby cabinet. "Also, it is not a date." He scoffed again, before scooping some food onto the flatware, handing a plate to her in the process. "Okay," she surrendered. "Since you don't believe me, what if you came along? Not only would it prove that it's not a date, but also you could get the opportunity to judge his character." He finally smiled for the first time since she walked in. She noticed the change in his demeanor and she playfully threw a tomato from her salad at him. "You know, I wouldn't be with someone you didn't approve of anyway."

"Sure, why not?" He laughed grabbing the fruit and popping it in his mouth. Maybe he would just tell Gia he's the worst and that would be it. No Diaz.

Days later, Campbell had weapons training with the same person he was concerned with. "Hey Diaz, come here." He straightly commanded. "Yes, Sergeant?" Diaz replied, placing his gun down and running over. "I been keeping an eye on you and I want you to come along with me on a job."

"Yes Sir." He smiled, excited for the chance to prove himself.

"So you saved Campbell. That is insane." Gia said with shock, before looking at her brother in bewilderment. "Yes, he did. Such a hero. He just jumped and tackled me down, saving me from a bullet. I am very glad that I can live to tell the tale." He muttered, dipping his fries in ketchup.

"Please. It really is no big deal. Saw a truck coming his way, and thinking he would get hit by a car, I just jumped by instinct. I didn't know there was a shooter at all in the vicinity." Diaz urged, shaking his hands in protest, awkwardly avoiding the praise. "I am sure if it was me, he would have done the same."

The same? I doubt it. If he was the one in front of the truck, I would have pushed him. Maybe tell everyone it was a tragedy, and chalked it up to destiny letting the truck deliver its justice. He was annoyed by his goody-two-shoes attitude, and he was getting ticked off by the blatant love eyes he was shooting Gia's way. "Right, well I think Gia has to be getting home now, it is a bit late." Campbell lied, standing up from his chair, before paying the bill.

I would never do the same. He is so absolutely undeserving.

—-

"You're right. And as her big brother, my only regret was allowing you to get close to her." He spat in anger. "John. I know you loved Gia. But she chose me. I am sorry that you were asked to be her family instead of her lover but that was her choice. Regardless of that, it doesn't excuse murdering women just to get back at me."

"Oh, you think I murdered those women just to get back at you? Not entirely. I didn't murder them. You did." He laughed. "What are you talking about?" Diaz cautiously asked. "You killed those women. Each and everyone one of them, waited and begged for Diaz to come to the rescue. And truly, you were late, as you always are." He maniacally added. "You can't do that. I didn't know where they were." Diaz insisted, blood pressure rising. "You killed them, just like you killed what family I had left, so now I will kill what family you have. I do apologize to Elijah's parents, they don't deserve this at all, no one should have to see family die. But such is life."

"No! Please, come on Campbell, shoot me. You don't have to kill him, just kill me!" He pleaded, scooting closer to the man in the chair. "No, I'm sorry. If I kill you, you will be happy.

I ended your suffering. But you don't deserve happy. I want you broken, with no chance of reversing that pain you will feel. As you see his mother cry, and his friends stricken with grief, knowing that it could have been avoided if you just got out of the way.

So say goodbye."

Campbell pointed the gun at Eli's temple, ready to pull the trigger as Diaz pleaded, begging him not to continue. He smirked and squeezed his hand on the cold steel.

Bang.

Blood spilled. Diaz quivered at the ringing sound, head hanging low, before getting the courage to look up slowly. What he saw surprised him. Campbell stared him in the eye, before his body slumped over, a singular gunshot wound piercing through his back. Diaz looked up in shock, higher than the body now riddling the ground, to see Q. wiping his gun and walking towards Elijah before kicking Campbell's body off of the sleeping young man.

"Sorry for the mess, but I did warn him. I kept telling Campbell that I don't like to share. Detective, Elijah is special, and I will tell you why." Mr. Q. lifted his mask, stunning Diaz. He couldn't believe the man in front of him was someone so close yet far away. "Shh. Don't spoil the fun. Or you, just like your brother and your wife will be dead. I mean it Detective."

"Why would you show me this? I don't understand." Diaz was genuinely afraid at this point. Q. wouldn't be showing this to him unless it meant he had something else under his sleeve. "This is a game of color, Detective. One that often ends with everyone bleeding." Q. sat on a chair, staring at the blood pooling closer to his shoes. "My identity was never hidden, it was just unimportant until now."

Diaz took a deep breath. "Why do you think I will listen to you?" "Because I have something very dear you want. Gia was dead. There was no bringing her back, unfortunately. But Rain comes and goes. Since the day I was there and saw as your wife held onto her last breath, fighting for your arrival. I knew you were unfit to be a father. So I took him."

"What do you mean?" Tears pricked Diaz's eyes. Hoping what Q. was insinuating was true. "My word, you're dim. But I am feeling generous today. I mean it is the least I can do for killing your brother here. Ex-brother-in-law I mean." Q. looked back at Eli. Then back at Diaz, smiling.

"Gosh you are so dim. Rain is alive. And well. Such a sweet little boy. On the day he was born, I simply switched him out with one of the dead ones."

Q. got up. Walking near the entrance, pausing before exiting the door. "If you don't keep your word. I will cause drought upon the land. If you get what I am saying. Tell Eli any of this, and you are dead, along with your soon-to-be five-year-old." He pushed the door open, walking out.

"Oh," Sticking his head back in. "Here's a parting gift." He slid a letter on the ground, it landing on the pile of blood in the middle of the room. "To color!"

Wisdom, let the games begin.

Resolutions

He's gone, Wisdom. "Mom hasn't stopped crying. I don't know what to do," Eli sighed into his phone, sharing his concerns with Daniel and Hope. "Do you want us to come over, maybe we can cook for a few days and she can get some rest for a while," Hope asked. Elijah was stuck. At least his friends were here with him. He was glad that they never resented him for going behind their backs and dealing with Q. alone. He should have told them, but then again he should have done a lot of things differently.

"Did you open the letter yet? Diaz called me about it yesterday. He's still waiting on your call." Daniel added. "No, I don't want to touch it. It keeps reminding me that all of this is real. That Campbell was evil, then he died, and now my Dad is dead too." Eli stared at the ceiling above him, wishing it would come crashing down. Life was becoming too much and he needed confirmation that everything was fake. That he would wake up thinking he had the nightmare of a lifetime.

"My mom can't take it." He sighed into the phone holding back his sadness. "My Dad was a great man, and it's my fault he is gone." "Come on E. You know that is not true. Your Dad is a hero, and yes he went to save you but that's not your fault. Any good parent would sacrifice themselves for their children.

All you have to do with everything going on, is to honor him and live well. That's all you owe anyone." Hope said trying to comfort her friend. "Thanks Hope, but we both know that if I didn't go try to investigate on my own, he would still be alive." Eli got up ignoring the letter that sat on his desk, pulling his things out of his hospital bag.

"I think I am done. You can call Diaz and tell him that. It may be too late, but I just want to help my mom now." He folded the last of his clothes and plopped back onto his bed, grabbing a crumpled t-shirt and hitting the light switch off with it.

"Alright. But call us if you need anything. You know we have your back, okay?" That's what I'm scared of Wis. Q. is still lurking around, and everyone I love is slowly getting torn from me by the repercussions of my decisions and actions. I am done. I lost and that's just it. I lost too much and I will not sacrifice anymore. Eli's phone rang again. He absentmindedly hit the answer button, picking it up, thinking his friends forgot to say something. "What's up?"

"Hey, Eli. I am sorry to call, I know you're friends told you I would wait but I need you to read that letter. Please." Diaz softly spoke through the speaker. "Please stop calling me. I mean I really don't get it! Why must I continue to get dragged into this? You won't even tell me why you keep pushing this. Or why you can't just do things like the police always do. Why do you keep pestering me Diaz? Nope. I am done. I hope you find what you are looking for. Bye Detective." He was about to hang up just as Diaz shouted in alarm. "Hey kid, I am sorry for your loss. I truly am. I know death is never easy to face but your Dad would not want you to just things quit halfway. That's not what a man does. Don't you want to avenge his goodness?"

"How would you know what my Dad thought?" He huffed

131

sitting up and speaking into the phone. "Even if what you say it true, it doesn't matter, he is gone and my mom is all I have left." "Fine then. Do this for your mom, who says Q. won't kidnap her again?" Diaz sighed into the phone. "Look I can't tell you why I am pushing this but you are a smart kid. You know me, and you know that this has to be for a good reason for me to push you like this. So just read the letter. And if after you read it, you still feel it's dumb to continue this, then I will leave you alone. But you have to man up and tell me that to my face. Deal?"

"I'll think about it." Eli declared. "And that's all I ask of you. Say hi to your mom for me. Bye, Elijah." Eli hung up the phone thinking about the events that occurred in the past week. There was that little voice in his mind egging him on to just see it through. But logic was telling him to hang up his junior detective gear and move on.

—-

When he awoke, he was in the Hospital, bruised and head pounding. Pain hit the front of his forehead as he tried to sit up, convincing him that it took too much energy to be moving so fast, so he laid back down. "Oh my gosh! Elijah, you scared me!" His mom hugged him softly as if he would break under her delicate touch. He hugged her back unsure of what was happening. "Mom, I'm okay. I'm here."

She let go of him partially and looked down at the floor. This alarmed him because whenever she did that she had bad news to share. Really bad news.

"What's going on, you are acting as if someone died?" He jokingly asked rubbing her hand. She bit her lip unsure of how to continue. "Eli, it's your Dad, son." "What's up with Dad? Speaking of him, where is he?"

"That's the thing. Your father loves you, you know that. And that day you went out, he felt as if something was off. So about an hour after you left, he checked your location and saw that you were at his job." The pacing of her storytelling made his heart race. She shifted in her seat.

"Yeah? Mom, you are scaring me. Tell me what happened next?" With a shaky breath, she continued. "Well, he left out to go see what you were up to. I thought it was nothing but young adults playing around. Thought maybe you were with your friends. To check, I called Hope and Daniel but they said they hadn't seen you all day. That didn't sound right to me so I rang your Dad but he didn't pick up either. I waited about two maybe three hours, with no one picking up the phone." Hearing this made him feel guilty, it wasn't right to make his mom panic like that.

"So I got in a taxi and went to the cab company myself. When I got there it was on fire, building crumbling before me. I asked the police what was going on and they said a bomb exploded." She began crying at this point and Eli felt worse for putting his mother through this pain. "I am really sorry Mom, I was just looking for clues. I didn't mean to worry you."

"That's not all Elijah." This frightened him. What else could be going on? "Your father was there. The police said that he must have been trying to find you in the rubble. They could not find a body but they found his teeth in the wreckage the next day indicating he was there." Eli's breath hitched, head feeling woozier than before.

"Your Dad," she whispered in a very hushed tone. "Died trying to save you." His mom was crying at this point, face stricken with sadness. "I know it is not your fault son. I just wish he was still here. I wish he knew you were safe."

Eli was stunned, the shock becoming too much, and he fell unconscious in his hospital bed, alerting his mom who called for the doctor, crying for help.

—-

A few days passed, and Eli was in the kitchen putting some food on a plate for his mom, who was too sad to eat on time. "Mom, your food is ready." He heard no response so he walked into his parent's room, hit with the familiar scent of his Dad's cologne wafting in the air. It hit him like a truck, imagining that he would walk out of the closet to ask which tie matched his shoes that day. But Eli knew that no one would emerge from the door. That there would be no fashion questions for a very long time. Holding back tears, he set the tray down on his mom's nightstand near the bed, helping her sit up to eat. "Mom, everyone pitched in for the funeral, and I invited Dad's coworkers to come. I just want you to know that Dad had a lot of friends. People that cared for him." She nodded shakily, weak from the dehydration of her grief. "That's good Eli, your father deserves that, and thank you for taking care of me these last few days. I don't know what to do without your Dad. It's so hard." She sniffled a bit grabbing a napkin to dry her tears. He patted her on the back before backing away and handing her a glass of water.

"Of course Mom, it's the least I can do." He left the memory filled room in silence, shutting the door behind himself and walking solemnly to his room. As he entered his scattered abyss, he spotted the envelope on his desk. He sighed knowing he would have to read it eventually and give Diaz a final answer. As he picked it up he noticed that it was covered in dried blood, Campbell's blood. 'I can't believe Q. killed him. All while I was knocked out. How crazy.'

He peeled it open trying not to get any residue on his hands, reading the lines below.

Dear Elijah,

This letter is more serious than the others so will I forego witty words and rhetoric.

I am sorry. This game was meant for two and now so many have been dragged into it. Unfortunately, along with everything else, your father is dead. I was not behind that untimely explosion and for that, I had to kill Campbell. I intended to bring you along my side amicably. He went against the rules and pulled in those unnecessary and innocent.

Elijah was angry, despite the apology, it felt as if Q. was stating that his Dad was just caught in the crossfire, a simple casualty. The audacity rubbed him the wrong way. He continued reading;

You see, this game was for Diaz and while you dragged yourself in, I had no intention of letting you get hurt or you soiling my plans. To be honest, you were an afterthought. An anomaly at best, but Campbell was colder than I remembered. We were children when we met and I guess I pitied his former self, instead of seeing the man in front of me. So for that, I am sorry. It was rather reckless of me.

But let us not get it twisted. You were never going to win. This story can have only one winner and from the moment you joined, you lost. I did advise you to stay away from Diaz because he has a lot he is willing to sacrifice. And for the reason that you shouldn't test fate, doing that to your poor mother.

I do think you should watch her better. Who knows? If you don't heed my words, I might have to stop by for some more of her delectable treats. She really is a fantastic baker. What a woman.

I am getting carried away. Elijah, my friend, you were never supposed to react. This is the consequence of doing more than life intended for you. Stay a bystander, there is no shame in survival.

May our paths never cross again,

Mr. Q.

P.S.

   In case you are foolish and decide to join up with Diaz. Then welp. I warned you. Let the games begin.

I am lost Wisdom. What am I to make of any of that? My Dad is dead and Q., somehow apologized and threatened me. What gives? Well. I promised Diaz I would talk to him. I should tell him that, especially, after this weird letter; that I am done. Eli threw the paper in the trash, washed his hands, and went to check on his Mom. When he cracked open her door, he saw that she was looking at a picture, crying. It was the one that was always on her nightstand, an image of Eli and his Dad at his high school graduation. They were so proud that he had won valedictorian. That was a good day, back when times were good.

   "Hey Mom, I have to go talk some more with the police about

everything. I will keep my phone on me during it all, and Daniel will come to check on you in a few." He assured her. "Okay, come back soon." She smiled softly through her sullen lips. He kissed her cheek and nodded. "Of course. It should only take thirty minutes tops, I promise."

—-

He walked into the Olive Branch and sat down ordering a hot chocolate. "I guess some things don't change," spoke Diaz sliding into the booth. "How are things kid?" "Not so good." Eli spoke truthfully, sipping his drink whilst he stared at the Detective in front of him. It struck Eli, that Diaz looked older, more tired and rundown. "You honestly look like you need some sleep."

"Yeah, I do. Been a rough few days." Diaz sighed. "Anyway, you here to turn me down?" already accepting defeat. "I am, but I am interested in hearing why you want to continue this sick game. What could be so important?" Diaz shook his head in silence, sliding a sheet of paper towards him, before grabbing the coffee he ordered, patting Eli on the shoulder, and heading out the door. "See you kid, call me if you need anything." Eli looked at the detective confusingly before turning his attention back to the paper, ignoring the bell of the entrance ring.

He has Rain, and just like that, I don't believe I burn everything around me. This all has simply been a simulation, a mere game and I don't want to be a pawn anymore. I see you as a son, E. But this is beyond that. He has all I ever wanted and all I have lost. I am probably going to die in the process of fighting Q. And I am willing to do that. This is for Gia, and those women, even for Campbell, and especially for your Dad. -Diaz.

He sat for a while after reading that paper. He wasn't even sure what he was thinking about or if he was considering Diaz's offer. He thought about his Dad and what he would go through if it was Eli in Rain's place. He imagined that he would be like Diaz in this situation. Never giving up on hope, and Eli knew what he had to do.

I am an idiot Wisdom. An idiot who can't say no. To be honest I don't think I was ever going to stay away. Not since everything is in Q.'s favor. I am a sore loser, a bystander, a powerful being who has stumbled on the most horrible story. A person who sees all and ultimately decides. Decide whether to quit and always regret, or stand up to what is right. So whatever Wis. I'm not the brightest anyway.

Let the games begin…again.

About the Author

Entel is an mystery author who enjoys all things suspense, science fiction, and wonder. After reading a few detective stories, they were struck with the idea to create a world where the watcher was the main point-of-view.

When not writing stories laced with plot twists, they find comfort in the small wonders of life, such as watching romantic comedies, reading fantasy novels, and creating new dishes in the kitchen.